DEATH AT THE ALTAR

An absolutely gripping murder mystery full of twists

NORMAN RUSSELL

An Oldminster Mystery Book 5

Joffe Books, London
www.joffebooks.com

First published in Great Britain in 2023

Cover art by Dee Dee Book Covers

ISBN: 978-1-80405-719-3

PROLOGUE

Hunched under the weight of a large bag, he scurried across the dark churchyard, dodging gravestones and stumbling over the uneven ground. The clouds hung low and heavy, unseasonably dark. The storm was about to break.

The church door opened at his touch — that put him on edge. No point in stealing a key if nobody had locked up. He stepped in and lugged the bag gratefully into a pew, then jumped as the door closed smoothly behind him and left him in darkness.

It had been broad daylight when the plan had come to him — the summer storm had taken him by surprise and he hadn't thought to bring a torch. He patted his pockets for his phone, then froze. The door was opening again.

Hastily he ducked behind a pew. The demon woman was on to him! There she was now, torchlight bobbing about. Looking for him? He held his breath.

Why, he wondered, didn't she just switch on the lights? She'd find him in a minute. Was it for the thrill of the chase? Or was it someone else who shouldn't be here? He frowned at the light, trying to make out the person holding the torch.

His persecutor didn't come his way, in fact the light had stopped quite close to the entrance. It played over the baptismal font, and then the person set down the torch for a moment and he saw their face. He hissed at the sight, then held his breath. But the person at the font didn't look round; they were intent on their task. Soon the deed was done, and the light bobbed out of the church.

He leant back against the pew, feeling triumphant that he had evaded detection. But what had he just witnessed? When his heart had recovered from the alarm, he summoned up all his courage and edged up to the font. For a brief moment, he pulled out his phone and lit up the room with his phone torch.

And gasped.

1. JOHN MILLER'S NARRATIVE:
A PARISH DIVIDED

In the summer of 2018, the Devil himself came to hold sway over our little village of Rushbrooke Hill, four miles south of the cathedral city of Oldminster. The people of Rushbrooke Hill are not particularly superstitious, but they were quite right in thinking that something particularly evil had got loose in the village.

The Devil — if it was the Devil — centred his activities on the ancient parish church of Holy Trinity, where first profanation, and soon afterwards a particularly vile murder, led to the church being closed by Bishop Poindexter of Oldminster, until he judged the time to be right for the building, and all other church buildings on the site, to be reconsecrated.

I have spent a lifetime fending off a tendency to cynicism, which I regard as a grave personal fault. Cynics do nothing but sneer at the actions of others, while failing to achieve much themselves. But when the Devil paid us that terrifying visit, I couldn't help thinking what a blow it would be for our neighbouring village of Staunton Maltravers, whose inhabitants for years have preened themselves on its Civil War ghosts, who apparently roam its streets at will. The annual 'ghost trail' has brought them a lot of visitors, and a general boost in income. Well, maybe we'll do something similar here at Rushbrooke Hill, and conduct tours of the place where the Devil reigned supreme for a time. But there: I really must guard against cynicism.

I am writing this account of what happened at the request of Bishop Poindexter, who wants a personal record of events from a parishioner to lodge in the cathedral archives, something written by an eyewitness to the appalling murder, to supplement the formal police records of the case, and I was only too willing to oblige.

The trouble is, that I can see this account turning into a kind of novel, the difference being that this particular story will be an account of true events. I once fancied myself as a novelist, and self-published a story set in the eleventh century. Nobody read it, and thankfully that particular youthful folly has been long forgotten.

I think the bishop chose me for the task because I had written two legitimate books many years ago, both of which are still in print. This in his eyes made me an author. Both books were on the pathology of the renal gland, written in my early years in practice, when I imagined that I might become a specialist, with consulting rooms in Chichester. In the event, I stayed put in Rushbrooke Hill, and have never regretted my decision to do so.

My name is Dr John Miller, proud to describe myself as a general practitioner. I am aged fifty-eight, and a lifelong resident of Rushbrooke Hill. For many years I have been organist at Holy Trinity, and an on-and-off member of the parochial church council, the PCC, in various positions over the years. I enjoy my work as the local GP in a small rural community. My surgery is in the front room of my house. And I am a familiar sight cycling around the village on my rounds. People *will* get ill, and women *will* have babies, so there's plenty for me to do. I am somewhat bald, and rather fat, and have a troubled conscience over my obesity.

I will begin this account by describing a meeting of the standing committee of the PCC. The purpose was to agree on the shortlist drawn up by the parish secretary, Alan Shirtcliffe, to appoint a new vicar, the church having been rudderless since the retirement of old Canon Harper some months before.

When Augustus Harper retired, civility and sanity retired with him, as you'll see. He was a level-headed man, with the ability to resolve disputes by a few carefully chosen words. He was seventy-five, and the Church authorities insisted that it was time for him to go. He didn't want to go, and we didn't want to lose him.

There's a wall plaque inside the church to an eighteenth-century vicar who died in office at the age of ninety-four. Those were the days! Anyway, the archdeacon, 'after much thought and prayer' — that's the kind of thing the hierarchs say — insisted on him going, so that was that.

It was on that day of the meeting, as it transpired, that the smoke of Satan began to seep through the ancient walls of Holy Trinity. Looking back now at all that happened subsequently, I don't think all my talk of Satan is simply a fanciful use of language.

There were seven members of the standing committee, four men and three women, and all were present at the meeting, which was held at eleven o'clock in the morning in the old lime-washed meeting room just off the west door of the church. Sitting there, you could hear the ponderous creaks and gasps emitted by the clock mechanism in the tower above us.

It was a nicely balanced committee, the kind of thing that Canon Harper approved of, representing different types of churchmanship. I myself am a peacemaker, tending to throw in my lot with the majority on most issues. Canon Harper used to say, 'I know you, John: anything for a quiet life.'

I had arrived early, and sat twiddling my thumbs until I heard the door open. Into the room came Colonel Nigel Calderdale, a handsome man with a luxuriant fair moustache and fierce penetrating blue eyes. He was wearing a sage-green tweed suit, and his white shirt was adorned with a red bow tie. Some people might take this sartorial preference as something that brands him as a survival from the 1950s, but this is hardly fair. Nigel was more than that, at least he was, until — well, I'll leave all that to later in my account.

Nigel Calderdale is by way of being the local squire. He resides in Rushbrooke House, an old property with its front entrance on the high street. The Calderdales have lived there for centuries, and have held the patronage of the living since 1854 — that means their family has funded the local church and chosen the local vicar since that time. Calderdale is four years younger than me, a retired regular army officer, and a local magistrate.

'Well, John,' said Nigel, 'today's the day! I'll be very interested to see who you've chosen for the shortlist. It's a pity that I don't have a real say in the choosing, and only get to see the list of names today. But there it is: we must go by the rules.'

'Still, Nigel,' I said, 'as patron you have to approve our final choice, and if you disagree, you have the right to veto the appointment.'

'Yes, yes, I know, but could you imagine me doing that? I'm supposed to keep the peace here, not stir up scandal. Anyway, it's not going to happen.'

Holy Trinity is a very 'High' church, easily mistaken for Roman Catholic, with several altars, statues and the use of great quantities of incense. One nineteenth-century vicar was actually imprisoned for seven days for refusing to remove a wooden tabernacle from the high altar, and we've always attracted what you might call the more enthusiastic members of the Anglo-Catholic societies, who come here on pilgrimage, as it were. Canon Harper would show them the grave of the imprisoned vicar in the churchyard, and they'd all sing the Roman Catholic hymn 'Faith of our fathers'.

Nigel Calderdale is — or was — a fanatical Papalist Anglo-Catholic, and we all knew that he would scrutinise the candidates very carefully, to make sure that they were 'sound'. He can be mulishly stubborn. He is a widower, and lives with his housekeeper, Ruth Page. Ruth's a good soul, who occasionally confides to me that she wished Holy Trinity was a bit more 'Anglican'.

Over the course of the next quarter of an hour the other members of the committee arrived. Alan Shirtcliffe was first. He's the parish secretary and vicar's warden, who by virtue of his office was *ex officio* chairman. Alan farms a thousand acres to the west of the village. A physically strong man with a shock of fair hair, he is in his mid-forties. In 'church-speak' Alan could be described as a 'liberal Catholic'. Colonel Calderdale, strict on dogma, often locks horns with Alan, though the two men have mutual respect for each other. I wondered what would happen when Nigel saw the shortlist.

Alan and his wife Megan have two young children, and she runs the church's mother and toddler group. Everybody likes Megan. She also happens to be an open supporter of women's ordination, which is still a divisive issue in Anglo-Catholic circles. She is not, thank goodness, a member of the PCC.

'Am I late?'

Tony Savidge, who is our indispensable garage mechanic, rushed into the vestry, nodded to Nigel, and sat down at the stout oak table. Tony is a Papalist, like Nigel, but I knew that he would always defer to the majority without fuss. He is a good, solid man, with a wife and four children. He is highly regarded for being able to bring our failing cars to life.

When Rose Talmadge arrived, I saw a subtle change in Nigel's stance. He treated her to a welcoming smile, and rose to set a chair for her. *Hello*, I thought, *there's more than meets the eye to all this old-world courtesy. Maybe Nigel's fed up with being a widower.*

Rose Talmadge, a retired teacher, is a brilliant gardener, who with a faithful band of helpers, tends the church gardens. She's a hundred per cent behind Nigel in everything, and is probably his staunchest ally. Maybe she'll be more than that one of these days. You'll have gathered now that I'm an inveterate gossip.

The others arrived within minutes. Amanda Waters is a solicitor, born and bred in Rushbrooke Hill. She had the great privilege of being delivered by me one stormy winter's night when her mother went into labour before the ambulance could arrive. Amanda once confided in me that she was beginning to feel a call to ordination, though nothing has come of that so far.

The last member to arrive, Sally Eardley, was also one of the most recent additions to the village. Sally is a good Church of England woman, the type who attends her parish church whatever its churchmanship. Some people find her standoffish, but I like her a lot.

It was time to open the meeting.

'We've come here this morning,' said Alan Shirtcliffe, 'to agree on the shortlist of three candidates for the vacant post of vicar. It's been reduced to three from the list of nine names suggested by the full meeting of the PCC last month. I'm hoping that this meeting will be a mere formality, so that we can arrange the interviews for Friday week.'

Alan handed each of us a sealed envelope, which we duly opened. There was a typed sheet of paper, listing the names and brief details of the candidates' careers. Two of the candidates posed no problems: they seemed to be two worthy men, of the right age, and with the right qualifications to be chosen as vicar of Holy Trinity. The third name, though, led to a few surprised murmurs.

I glanced at them all as they read the names. Tony Savidge pulled a face, and glanced at Nigel Calderdale, who was beginning to work up one of his red flushes. Rose Talmadge said nothing, but she, too, flushed, and sat grim and tight-lipped. Amanda looked thoughtful. I sensed that Sally Eardley was mildly amused. I, of course, retained my usual sphinx-like calm.

Nigel stood up, and waved his sheet of paper at us. I always thought that it was only in stories that a man's eyes flashed, but Nigel's were flashing now.

'There are three names here,' he said, 'two of them admirable, well-qualified men to fulfil the role of vicar here at Holy Trinity. I see that one of them was trained for the priesthood at St Stephen's House, Oxford, and was at St Saviour's, Haggerston, for a while. And the other has served curacies in some very well-known Anglo-Catholic parishes. The third — well, I assume that name's there to pacify the rural dean? Very keen on priestesses, is Mr Verity. Well, I'll say no more about that, but I want to remind you of my own position in this matter. Warn you, would be a better way of putting it.

'As patron of the living, I am not a member of the PCC, and I don't have a vote in this matter. But I *do* have the right of presentation, and no one can be appointed vicar without my consent.'

'Hear, hear,' muttered Rosamund Talmadge, and was rewarded with a grateful glance.

Now you may find it surprising that nobody spoke up at this childish outburst of Nigel's. I'm afraid we had seen something of it before, and by far the safest way of dealing with it is to ignore it. I saw Sally and Amanda exchanging a quick grin at the tantrum — it was lucky Nigel didn't spot them or things might have escalated. As it was, our lack of response rather took the wind out of his sails.

'Your position is noted, Nigel,' said Alan mildly. 'Now, as to the voting members, may I take it that the list is approved? Please can we have a show of hands?'

Rather to my surprise, all hands, including Nigel's, were raised, and it was agreed that the interviews would take place on Friday week.

As the meeting dispersed, I heard Nigel say, 'Don't worry, Rose, that third name is the rural dean's doing. Anyway, I've made my position quite clear. It ought to be plain sailing.'

I joined Alan Shirtcliffe as we left the church and walked down the village high street towards the market cross, where he had parked his big Land Rover.

'I wouldn't like to be in your shoes next week, Alan.' I laughed. 'Nigel's not going to take this lying down.'

'I'm not so sure,' said Alan. 'He and I have had some almighty rows about church matters in the past, but we've always managed to remain friends.'

I had very strong doubts about that, and of course I was right. Remember what I said about the smoke of Satan?

When I got home, I sat down at the kitchen table and re-read the resumé of our chosen candidate that Alan had given me at the meeting. The Reverend Stacey Williams was eminently able, with what Nigel would have called a 'sound' background in Anglo-Catholic ministry. Not many obscure country churches would be presented with such a highly qualified candidate for the post of vicar.

Stacey Williams was unmarried, but despite this recommendation to the various Papalist factions of the Church of England, she belonged to the quietly thriving liberal group known as Affirming Catholicism. A bit of an enigma there, then, but in every way a top-notch choice for Holy Trinity. That is, if a miracle happened, and Nigel Calderdale raised no objections.

The two men on the shortlist were good, reliable candidates, both in their fifties, and with plenty of life left in them. All three candidates had supplied sheaves of references. Which way would things go? Only one thing was certain. The rural dean had had nothing to do with the choice, as Nigel seemed to think. That list was *our* list, arrived at after long and sober discussion. Nigel might soon find himself with an almighty fight on his hands.

2. JOHN MILLER'S NARRATIVE:
THE DEMONS UNLEASHED

Colonel Calderdale, the patron, as custom demanded, was not present at the interviews of the candidates. The committee would acquaint him with their decision as soon as it was made, and we would send someone to fetch him from Rushbrooke House to give his assent as patron, and meet the successful candidate. The three hopefuls were sitting in the clergy vestry at the other end of the church, pretending not to hate each other.

Amanda Waters acted as the messenger, ferrying the candidates into our presence one after the other. They were told that we had made our choice, and the losers took it in good part, while the winner observed a sort of grave silence. Amanda ushered them all back to the vestry, and stayed with them. Her job now was to get rid of the losers, and keep the winner safe until she was summoned into Nigel's presence.

Sally Eardley volunteered to fetch Nigel, and we sat there waiting for her to return. Alan Shirtcliffe was looking particularly intrepid, as though preparing himself for a verbal showdown of some sort. Tony Savidge appeared studiously neutral. Rose Talmadge sat with compressed lips, her eyes fixed on the table. She is a handsome woman, and that kind of expression does nothing for her general attractiveness. Sally Eardley, our recent 'import' from London, looked vaguely amused. Evidently she had never experienced the kind of unholy bust-ups that are fairly frequent in church gatherings of this sort.

As for me, well, I was a hundred per cent behind Alan Shirtcliffe on this occasion, though as always I'd try to pour oil on troubled waters if things got out of hand.

After what seemed an age, Amanda and Colonel Calderdale came into the vestry, and took their seats at the table. I was expecting instant shenanigans, but Nigel was looking particularly happy, greeting us all with a smile.

'So, friends,' he said, 'we are to have a new vicar at last! I'm intrigued as to which of the two you've chosen. They both seemed eminently suitable, loyal to the Catholic tradition, and with excellent references. Father MacLeod had the edge over Father Roberts, I thought, but that's just my opinion. So, which of them have you chosen?'

Alan Shirtcliffe sat back in his chair and glanced around at us all. I saw the little tremor at his temple, always a warning sign that he was stoking up reserves of strength for any opposition from the patron. He picked up a sheet of paper from the table, glanced at it, and then put it down again. I think we all held our breaths.

'Well, Nigel,' said Alan in a sort of pacific, coaxing tone, 'we wanted to choose the best candidate, and that's what we did — five for, and one against. In our view, by far the best candidate was the one we've chosen — the Reverend Stacey Williams.'

Colonel Nigel Calderdale didn't just flush red with anger, he began to quiver with rage. I thought he was going to have a stroke. Rose Talmadge began to whimper, and Sally Eardley whispered something soothing to her. Nigel got to his feet.

'This is too bad, Alan,' he said, choking with rage. 'You know quite well that I will not accept a so-called female vicar as incumbent or curate here. They're an egalitarian fad, nothing to do with religion, and all to do with left-wing chicanery and so-called "women's lib". Are the candidates still here in the vestry? Go there now, and offer the living to one of those men.'

Alan spoke quietly, but with a settled determination that showed he was not to be bullied or intimidated.

'I'm sorry, Nigel,' he said, 'but we have made up our minds. The Reverend Stacey Williams is highly qualified, has glowing references, and is very much respected in more liberal Anglo-Catholic circles. We are asking you, as patron, to give your formal consent to the appointment. Then we can have her in here for you to meet—'

'Meet be damned! I will never meet this woman. She is no more a priest than I am.'

'That's a matter of opinion,' said Amanda Waters hotly. It was the first time I'd heard her contradict Nigel Calderdale. 'The arguments against women being priests are based on misogyny, and nothing else.'

'Nonsense, you silly girl,' cried Rose Talmadge. 'Our Lord chose only men as his apostles. We've managed without women at the altar for two thousand years.'

'Managed, but not flourished,' said Sally Eardley. 'Times change, Rose, and the Church must change with them, or fade away.' There were a few hesitant murmurs of agreement. A line of Tennyson came into my mind: 'The old order changeth, yielding place to new'.

Nigel had mastered his anger, though I could see that he was still inwardly fuming. He stretched out a hand and quite unselfconsciously took Rose's in his.

'Dear Rose,' he said. 'Always strong in the faith, and a dear, loyal friend. I've no doubt that it was you who voted against this — this monstrosity.'

Rose blushed with pleasure. It wasn't like Nigel to use such tender language, and I wondered again whether there was something brewing between those two.

'You more or less agreed to abide by our decision last week,' said Alan. 'So will you authorise Stacey Williams to be the next vicar?'

'No, I will not.'

Nobody said anything, though I heard Sally Eardley mutter, 'Crikey!' under her breath. I envisioned a hideous scandal, with Nigel locking horns with the archdeacon, the diocesan chancellor and Bishop Poindexter himself. The scandal would not be contained here in Oldshire. The national press and other media would be on to it in a flash.

'However,' said Nigel Calderdale, 'there is a way out of this impasse. I can't prevent you from going to the Devil in your own way, if that's what you want to do. My family have been patrons of this living since the 1850s. Nevertheless, I will now formally renounce my patronage, and confer it temporarily on you, Alan. It'll take a few days for the paperwork to go through, but you can act as patron from this moment.'

'That's — that's enormously generous of you, Nigel,' said Alan, his voice faltering.

'It's the only way out of this ridiculous deadlock. I wish you joy of your priestess. I've worshipped in this church all my life, but I shall never enter it again while that woman is in charge. I'll drive into Oldminster on Sundays, and go to St Agatha's, where Father Fielding keeps the old faith alive.'

Colonel Nigel Calderdale looked at Rose Talmadge.

'Fancy coming home with me, Rose?' he said. 'We can have a spot of lunch together.'

And so Nigel Calderdale left Holy Trinity with never a backward glance, and Alan brought the Reverend Stacey Williams up from the vestry to tell her that she had been appointed vicar of Holy Trinity, Rushbrooke Hill.

Nigel Calderdale had been shaken to the core at the PCC's decision, and yet, through all the anger, the man's fundamental decency had shone through. He had transferred his office of patron to Alan Shirtcliffe rather than leave his beloved Holy Trinity rudderless and racked by scandal.

Nigel phoned me that afternoon. 'Look here, John,' he said, 'you're my GP, and my friend. I'd be grateful if you'd keep me informed about what goes on in the parish — what people are saying, that kind of thing.'

I agreed. It seemed the decent thing to do.

* * *

As I approached Holy Trinity church for the induction of our new vicar, I was alarmed to see a small crowd had formed just outside the church gates. I spotted Amanda Waters standing at the back of the group and joined her.

'Anything amiss?' I asked.

'Pitchforks at dawn,' she answered, nodding ahead. And now I realised that most of the crowd were there to gawp at three strangers who had blocked off the gates with a couple of placards and a table of leaflets.

'"Bible says no!",' Amanda read off the placard, and fluttered a leaflet at me that she must have picked up from the table. 'Not very eloquent, I'm afraid, but their point is clear.'

'No female vicars?'

'Our place is in the pews.' She smiled at me but I could tell she was upset. 'It must be twenty years since women were first ordained. Will this hatred ever end?'

At that moment a car drove up and a young cleric hopped out with alacrity — probably someone checking the way was clear for the suffragan bishop. He was obviously more used to this sort of thing than us.

'Now then, Reverend Stringer!' he called out. 'And Mr Vholes, if I'm not much mistaken? You've had your protest but you're blocking a right of way. Move it over to the side a bit. Or do you want to prevent all these people from communing with God?'

The crowd murmured in approval and shuffled forward expectantly; in fact, it morphed from a crowd into a queue to get through the gate. The red-faced protestors complained about their right to protest and suchlike, but in the face of an Englishman's blocked right of way they didn't stand much of a chance and soon protestors and placards alike were brushed aside.

'So that's the great anti-female resistance,' I remarked to Amanda as the protestors packed their signs away. 'They don't seem all that much to be worried about.'

I was wrong, of course, I see that now. The Devil gets into a place in all kinds of ways and through all kinds of people.

* * *

The Reverend Stacey Williams was formally inducted to the living by the Right Reverend Michael Sandford, the Suffragan Bishop of Bedworth, himself only recently appointed. The church was packed that evening, partly because local people wanted to see this curiosity, a rarity in their part of the world, a female vicar.

They saw a handsome, unselfconscious woman who bore herself with great dignity as she was led to the altar, the pulpit and the west door, where she was handed the keys of the church. She made a brief address to the congregation in a firm, well-trained voice, saying how thrilled she was to be starting a new ministry here.

'To grow we have to change,' she said, 'and face up to the challenges of this post-modern era. Let us do this together, honouring and preserving all that was best in the past, while looking outward to the wider world, and what we can do to make it a better place to live in.'

It was customary, she went on, in Anglo-Catholic churches to address the vicar as 'Father'. However, she felt that to be addressed as 'Mother' was the prerogative of a Mother Superior, and that she would be content to be addressed as 'vicar', or just plain Stacey. I relayed all this to Nigel over the phone that evening. 'It's the beginning of the rot,' he said. 'When that type of woman says "change" she means "destruction". You'll see, John, she will destroy everything that we stand for.'

* * *

After Stacey had moved into the vicarage, she invited Alan Shirtcliffe and me to morning coffee. She had also sent Nigel an invitation, but he had not deigned to reply. She had furnished the vicarage well, so that it had all the informal comfort of a home, even though there were a number of boxes still waiting to be unpacked. There were large, comfortable sofas covered in chintz, mahogany bookcases, and an evidently cherished harmonium. There were lots of books and magazines about, but no sign of a TV. Perhaps she kept that in her study at the back of the house.

Stacey Williams had brought a housekeeper with her, a rather faded woman called Melanie Grint. She was a defeated sort of person of about thirty-five or so, who disliked making eye contact. That first day I met her she was dressed neatly in black dress and wrap-over apron, and I never saw her wear anything more glamorous than that. She was a good housekeeper and cook, so the vicar said, and she was obviously going to be a mainstay of the vicarage. I wondered whether the Reverend Stacey had rescued her from somewhere or other, and taken her under her wing.

Stacey greeted Alan warmly, though it was soon evident that it was me she wanted to see. She thanked me for my work as organist, and talked knowledgeably about church music as we sipped our coffee. And then she began to talk about the choir.

'They're valiant souls, aren't they?' she said. 'I was listening to them during the induction service. Only six of them, and all well advanced in years. Are you happy with them?'

'Well,' I said, 'they lead the hymns with something like gusto considering their years, and they sing the propers of the Eucharist clearly, as you'll hear this coming Sunday.'

'Hm . . . But I wonder whether it's not a good time for the parish to be more relatable for young people? I'd like to see a larger choir, with many more young people in it, and to get that, you've got to expand and modernise the repertoire. Could we not have a worship group, as a change from the organ?'

Alan seemed very struck with this idea. What he said next showed that he'd been thinking along the same lines, though he's never mentioned the matter to me.

'The RCs have got a marvellous group at Sacred Heart,' he said. 'I was speaking to Father Keegan the other week, and I know that he'd be only too happy to advise us, if we asked him.'

I was startled, to say the least! I was wondering what I would say to my coterie of elderly ladies and gentlemen as we were swamped by kids from the parish youth club.

'It's certainly something to think about, Vicar,' I said. 'I suppose you'd want to get rid of me too?'

The Reverend Stacey laughed, and shook her head.

'Not at all, John,' she said. 'I'm sure you'll be willing to embrace change, and lead the new choir to fresh triumphs once we've established it.'

It was all very civilised, particularly as I'm incapable of working myself up into a passion about anything. But it was the first chill wind of change, and I had an uneasy feeling that we had perhaps made a mistake in appointing her, not because she was a woman, but because she was going after change too quickly.

* * *

Stacey comported herself with great dignity on her first Sunday. Like her predecessor, she preferred to celebrate facing the east, with her back to the people. I saw that she said some prayers privately, bending low over the chalice and paten. I very soon forgot that she was a woman — well, hardly that, but you know what I mean.

At the conclusion of the service, she stood in front of the statue of Our Lady and sang the Angelus beautifully. It was, I thought, exactly the type of service Nigel Calderdale would have approved of.

* * *

The Reverend Stacey was a fast mover. The new choir was up and running within days of her arrival and, ever the peacemaker, I went along with it, teaching myself and the twelve boys and girls whom Stacey had rounded up from the local schools the 'worship songs' that the vicar had brought for me. Some of them were quite good, others were awful. The songs, I mean, not the boys and girls. My poor old cantors had been rather unceremoniously pensioned off, as it were; two of them joined Nigel Calderdale on his Sunday trips to St Agatha's in Oldminster. The others clung on grimly, and on the day the new choir performed at the Sunday service, they sat in enjoyable martyrdom in the back row of the pews.

Like Nigel, our new vicar referred to the Eucharist as 'the Mass', and it was abundantly clear to me that her theology on that point was one hundred per cent Papalist. I began to feel a growing resentment against Nigel for turning his back on us all at Holy Trinity. At the same time I was aware of the emergence of two camps, the pro-Stacey and the anti-Stacey, dividing the congregation. That was the Devil's doing.

The worship group never quite materialised while Stacey was with us, but another of Stacey's innovations was more successful. We had always had trouble getting boy servers for the Sunday Eucharist, though during the week a couple of old chaps would serve, tottering up and down the altar steps. Stacey introduced girl servers, and in no time had found and trained a team of twelve- and thirteen-year-olds, kitted them out in cassock and surplice, and let them loose on the altars. They were first class, very devout without fuss, and a great addition to Holy Trinity. A few more people left — Stacey said that this was known technically as 'punishing the vicar by deserting God'. When Nigel heard about the girl servers, he went incandescent.

It was after Stacey declared on the following Sunday that she intended to remove the old pews to create an expanded 'worship space' that somebody threw a brick through the vicarage window. It was the first attack of an unholy war — us against Satan. Satan won.

* * *

I called on the Reverend Stacey the day after the brick-throwing. The local handyman was already there, replacing the broken panes. Although she didn't realise it, the whole village was up in arms. The local bobby from Newton Ferrars had come to conduct an investigation, and had found everybody anxious to assist him in his enquiries. Various skulking strangers had been seen in the vicinity of the vicarage at different times of day and night. People had heard the smashing of glass on just about every evening of the week. The local delinquent had a sound alibi for the evening of the attack. The bobby's visit was much appreciated, but the culprit was not discovered.

Nigel Calderdale had phoned me at breakfast.

'This is an absolute disgrace, John,' he said. 'I just hope you'll believe me when I say that that act of vandalism was none of my doing. I can't wait for that woman to leave, but I'll never stoop to cads' tricks to drive her away.'

Nigel always used this kind of language, inherited from his late father. Nigel in his lifetime had encountered all kind of cads and rotters. I relayed his remarks to Stacey, who received them with a sad smile.

'I've only seen him once,' she said. 'It was in the high street, near the post office. We looked at each other, and he mumbled something and raised his hat before scurrying away. No, not "scurrying". That was unkind. He just hurried away. Well, I can't see Colonel Calderdale as a brick-thrower.'

'How are you?' I asked.

We were sitting in her study overlooking the vicarage garden. There was a large roll-top desk, a bookshelf crammed with religious works and an Apple iMac sitting on a card table. There was a large crucifix on the wall and a number of icons. Sitting on the mantelpiece was a statue of the Infant of Prague.

'I'm all right,' said the Reverend Stacey. 'It's not very nice, especially as Melanie and I are alone here most evenings.' Another smile, this one at some inner amusement as she added, 'My mother tells me I need a man about the place.'

Melanie Grint came in, bearing two mugs of tea. As always, she avoided looking either of us in the eyes. I wondered what her history was. I was sure that Stacey must have rescued her from some wretched fate or situation, but we had not known each other long enough for me to find out what! But I'm nothing if not nosy.

'I've had letters, too,' said the vicar when Melanie Grint had gone. 'Just recently. Five of them, all written in block capitals. One told me to "get out or else". Another simply said "Die, Witch!". One of them could not be read out to a respectable man like you, Doctor. Another one threatened to burn the church down if I didn't leave at once. And the fifth one read simply, "Thou shalt not suffer a witch to live." That's from Exodus, chapter twenty-two.'

I was appalled. There are about 750 people living in this village, and as the local doctor I know a great many of them. I just couldn't imagine any of these good folk writing poison pen letters. It was like something out of an Agatha Christie novel, only this was in the real world, and in deadly earnest.

'Did you give them to the constable when he called?' I asked.

'No. I burnt them all.'

I saw her expression change to one of dogged determination. I saw her glance at the crucifix, and then at the Infant of Prague, and her lips moved in a swift, silent prayer.

'And I will not be driven out of this parish by people with warped minds. I can manage a grudging respect for those who sincerely oppose us women priests — people like Colonel Calderdale and Rose Talmadge. They're a different matter entirely. But not these sad unbalanced people, skulking in the dark. Do you know the psalm verse "*negotium perambulans in tenebris*"? It comes in psalm ninety-one.'

She joined her hands together, and began to quote from the psalm.

'"Thou shalt not be afraid for any terror by night, nor for the arrow that flieth by day; For the pestilence that walketh in darkness: nor for the sickness that destroyeth in the noon day." That is my enemy, John: the pestilence that walketh in darkness, or in Latin, *negotium perambulans in tenebris*. And with God's help I will overcome that pestilence.'

What a fool Nigel Calderdale was to turn his back on this cultured, learned woman! If only he knew it, they had so much in common, a shared love of Catholic doctrine and practice as understood in the Church of England, and a measure of learning not always found in all the clergy. I realised that I had come to accept her and her ministry without question.

'Thank you for calling, John,' she said. 'I must get on with my parish visits. Don't worry about us. Melanie and I are tougher than we look. I'll see you on Sunday, God willing.'

Melanie Grint stopped me in the hall as I was on my way out. She addressed her remarks to the hall stand, unconsciously wringing her hands together as she spoke. I thought she looked careworn, and feeling a fear that she was determined to conceal.

'Doctor,' she said, 'if these people think they can drive the vicar out of her living, they're mistaken. She's left parishes because of persecution before, to keep the peace, and she's tired of it. She's a strong-willed woman, and utterly fearless. Now she has made up her mind, nothing will shift her. Here we are, and here we stay.'

'Did you hear any of these letters being delivered? I assume they were just put through the letterbox, not posted.'

'That's right. They came all at once, all five of them. That day, I'd walked out to Hinton's farm to buy some farm-cured bacon and black puddings — the vicar and I both like good, old-fashioned food — and when I came back, there they were, on the hall mat. She burnt them all for the rubbish, and I don't blame her. I tell you, Doctor, she's stronger than the lot of them!'

* * *

The day after that I made a professional call on Nigel Calderdale, who had developed a stye on his left eyelid. It was my first visit to Rushbrooke House since the appointment of Stacey Williams as vicar. It was a lovely old place, with ancient panelling in the soothingly dim rooms. There were a number of grandfather clocks, all ticking away solemnly, and chiming in a gentle old-fashioned way. Ruth Page, Nigel's housekeeper, kept everything polished and fragrant. Before all the trouble began, we would gather in Nigel's parlour once a week to talk about parish affairs as Nigel's guests: Alan Shirtcliffe, forever talking about his two little children and what they had said and done during the week; Tony Savidge, who cared for Nigel's old Bentley; and Rose Talmadge, not the grim opponent of the vicar, but a witty and much-loved member of the community.

There had been no such meetings since the Reverend Stacey Williams had been installed as vicar of Holy Trinity.

Nigel Calderdale looked under the weather. He seemed to have lost all his usual jauntiness. I treated his stye with golden eye ointment, and wrote him a prescription for antibiotics. When he offered me a glass of sherry, I accepted, though I don't usually drink in the mornings. He had always confided in me, and it was evident that he had something to tell me.

'John,' he said, 'I was visited the other day by a marvellous man called the Reverend Julian Stringer, representing a society opposed to women's ordination. He had heard about the fuss and bother that we've had here at Holy Trinity, and asked me to join the society that he had established. It's called the Warriors of Christ.'

I groaned inwardly. Hobnobbing with the likes of the Reverend Julian Stringer would drive Nigel further into the morass of obscurantism from which I hoped he had been emerging.

'He's coming here again this morning, at twelve,' said Nigel. 'I hope you'll stay to hear what he has to say. He's one of these very learned men with a vast knowledge of the whole business of ministry. Will you stay?'

I readily agreed. Nigel had whetted my curiosity about the founder of the Warriors of Christ.

He arrived just as the grandfather clocks were striking twelve. He was one of the protestors from the church gate — I thought I'd heard the name somewhere before. Stringer was a man in his sixties, dressed in black, and with the type of dog collar favoured by Roman Catholic priests. He was a thin, spare man, with long, cold fingers and restless eyes. When he talked, a little froth of bubbles would form at the corners of his mouth. I took an instant dislike to him. What was he doing, muscling in on another priest's territory? But then, like Nigel, the Reverend Julian Stringer didn't believe that Stacey was a priest at all.

'I explained to you last time, Colonel,' he began, 'that this woman, like all her kind, is a most dangerous energumen, planted here in your parish to be a destroyer of souls.'

'I beg your pardon, Father,' I said, 'but could you explain what that word means? Energumen.'

'Yes, indeed, Doctor. An energumen is a person possessed by the Devil, or one of his ancillary spirits. They were recognised in the Early Church, and were made the subject of exorcisms in order to drive the Evil One from them. That is the purpose of the Warriors of Christ. We go from parish to parish where these women have established themselves, and warn the people of the dangers they are facing. Colonel Calderdale had shown himself valiant for truth, which is why I am asking him to join the Warriors, and initiate a spiritual campaign to drive this energumen from your parish.'

Nigel said he'd give the matter serious thought, and soon afterwards the Witchfinder General left.

'A fascinating man, very sincere,' said Nigel, but he failed to meet my eyes, and seemed to shrink back on his chair. I'm not a psychiatrist, but I know enough on the subject to realise that my old friend's character was beginning to disintegrate. If the Devil was on walkabout, then he was to be found here, in Rushbrooke House, and not in Holy Trinity vicarage.

I thought that man was a lunatic. His ranting nonsense would have seemed silly had it not been so potentially dangerous. Something demonic was definitely in the air. The village was divided in its loyalties, and numbers had fallen in the congregation. I intended to support Stacey Williams as much as I could, but I began to long for the old, settled days when Canon Harper was vicar.

And then we were visited by a truly satanic incident which brought the bishop and the archdeacon scurrying from Oldminster to visit the site of the abomination, and got Rushbrooke Hill into the national newspapers. This is what happened.

3. JOHN MILLER'S NARRATIVE:
UNHOLY COMMUNION

It was a quiet weekday when Stacey performed her first baptism at Holy Trinity. The baptismal party was small — parents, grandparents, godparents and baby. They gathered at the font, which is near the west door, and Stacey came in from the vestry at the east end, wearing the customary surplice and stole. The stone font, elaborately carved, dates back to the days before the Reformation. No one these days uses the vast stone bowl. Instead, a decent glass bowl stands in the font, at that moment covered by a small white linen towel. Stacey formally asked for the child's name, which was Julie, and prepared to crook the baby in one arm, leaving the other arm free to pour water over her head.

She reached into the font, and removed the linen towel.

The glass bowl was full of thick, warm blood.

'What did you do?' I asked her, when I answered her frenzied phone call later that day.

'I nearly fainted! It was horrible — obscene. I could smell the blood, which had splashed over the side of the bowl and on to the stone base of the font. I had to drop the cloth back over the font quickly so that nobody in the baptismal party spotted it. I told them that I had decided to perform a very special baptism for Julie, and led them up to the high altar. There they stood while I hurried to the vestry, filled another bowl with some holy water that I kept in a flagon there, and returned. I baptised baby Julie at the altar, which pleased the party very much, though it is something very irregular that I'd never done before, and will never do again.'

'You called the police, I hope?'

'Oh, yes,' she said. 'This was a profane and blasphemous act, which I've no intention of leaving uninvestigated.'

'But surely we know who it must be?' I asked. 'Blood in a Christian church — that's surely the work of pagans?'

She knew who I was talking about, of course. Rushbrooke Hill might seem very dull and ordinary to an outsider, but we have all sorts here. Not least the Fellowship of Capricorn. I call them pagans for want of a better term — they are a cult of personality centred around an irritating man who insists on wearing awkward robes that trip him up wherever he turns. He calls himself the Master of the Goat Herd and talks a lot of nonsense about vibrations and electrosmog. I wouldn't put it past him to steal the church key and attempt to hold a Black Mass in the witching hour.

Stacey sighed. 'I won't deny I've had my run-ins with the fellowship, and I'd be delighted to bring them to the closer attention of the police, but I'm sure someone in the village would have seen something if it was a group. They would have made more of a mess, too.'

'Drag marks where they'd got blood on their robes?'

'That sort of thing. I hope the police question them, despite my doubts. I've also phoned the archdeacon. You see, I'm not sure whether the church will have to be reconsecrated, or at least blessed by the bishop, before things can return to normal.'

It was impossible not to admire her courage and determination, and I said as much. After we'd spoken I went straight to Rushbrooke House, and told Nigel Calderdale what had happened. He collapsed into a chair, and held his head in his hands.

'I never wanted anything like this,' he said in a small, shocked voice. 'This is vile beyond imagining. *Blood*? Who could have put it there? And where did it come from?'

'That's for the police to find out,' I said. 'Look, Nigel, will you go to see her, and tell her how sorry you are? A man of your distinction shouldn't be in the same camp as this ignorant mob of misogynists. These are the kind of people who used to burn witches in less enlightened times.'

'No, I won't see her. I'm sorry for what happened, but I won't be lured into Holy Trinity by false sentiment. I want that woman out of here. You remember what that clergyman said about energumens—'

I snorted with disgust, and left him to his solitary musings.

* * *

It turned out to be pig's blood.

On Saturday morning an old acquaintance of mine came out from Oldminster to conduct an investigation. Detective Inspector Paul French is a fellow member of the Oldshire Bridge circle, and we meet a few times a year at the bridge competitions held in Oldminster town hall. French likes to dress formally in a pin-striped suit, a white shirt and a Police Federation tie. He wears old-fashioned rimless glasses. It was French who solved the murders that occurred at the late Lady Renfield's birthday party, and the awful business of the killing in the cathedral library, among other cases. His reputation stands high, and I was pleased to see that he thought our disgusting mystery worth his personal attention.

'It's partly Bishop Poindexter's doing, John,' he said. 'He made an appeal to me, and I felt I couldn't refuse. It sounds like an evil prank, though. I don't swallow all this business of demons and devils. A personal vendetta, rather than part of a conspiracy to drive this lady out.'

'*Negotium perambulans in tenebris*,' I muttered, and he gave me a strange look.

'I'm going to the church now, to cast a professional look over things. You're the organist there, aren't you? Perhaps you'd like to come with me?'

It was a shock to see the whole area around the font sealed off with blue and white crime scene tape. I thought French would begin his investigation there. Instead, he began to wander around the nave, peering at the pews, and occasionally wiping his hand across them before examining his palm.

'It's a lovely church, isn't it?' he said. 'Very well maintained. I suppose the roof is watertight?'

'The roof? It certainly is. In fact, it was given a thorough overhaul this time last year.'

'Is the church locked during the day?'

'It's never locked,' I said. 'It remains open day and night, so that people can say a prayer or seek refuge there. Canon Harper insisted on that, and so does the Reverend Stacey.'

'Hmm . . . There was some fuss, I gather, over the patron refusing to present this lady as vicar? He resigned, didn't he?'

'Yes, sort of — he signed over his role to the parish secretary, but only by power of attorney. It's an ancestral role. If he wanted to give up the patronage for all time, he would have to jump through a few more hoops, I expect. Nigel Calderdale is very much opposed to women priests.'

'Opposed enough to try to frighten her away?'

'No, Nigel's not like that. He's as stubborn as a mule, but he's — well, he's a gentleman, if you know what I mean by that.'

Privately, I was beginning to think that Nigel's gentility was beginning to fray at the edges.

'So who's the patron now — this parish secretary you mentioned?'

'A man called Alan Shirtcliffe. He's quite a substantial farmer in this area.'

'I see. I brought a young constable down here with me today. He's out in the village now, making house-to-house enquiries — he'll gather statements from all these people.'

'Are you going to look at the font now?' I asked.

'The font? No, I don't think so — SOCO's done all that. But do you see these pews? Someone has sprinkled water across them, water that hasn't quite dried yet. How do you account for that?'

'I can't,' I replied. 'Now, if it had been Sunday today, the vicar would begin the Mass with what we call the Asperges, which involves her sprinkling the congregation with holy water. But not on a Saturday.'

'I'm not well up on these matters,' said DI French. 'How does holy water differ from ordinary water?'

'For a start, it's been blessed.' I tried not to look too annoyed at his chuckle. French is a first-class bridge player, but his spiritual imagination and sensitivity clearly leave something to be desired.

'I meant more along the lines of: does its chemical make-up differ to, say, tap water?'

'Well, there are a few different types of holy water. Some types have oil added to the mixture. Another type has a certain amount of salt added to it.'

DI French stooped down over one of the pews, and I saw him dip his finger in one of the small pools of water that had gathered there.

'Yes,' he said, 'this water tastes salty. Unless I'm very much mistaken, someone had been sprinkling holy water around here. Maybe the Reverend Stacey did it, to drive away evil.'

But Stacey, when I phoned her at the vicarage, stated quite firmly that she had done no such thing. Her own supplies of holy water were still intact.

The solution to this little mystery was not long in coming. A young, rather boyish uniformed constable came into the church, and was introduced to me as PC Gaunt.

'Well, Gaunt,' said DI French, 'any luck?'

'Yes, sir. When I called on the folk living in that little row of cottages opposite the church, I talked to an old man who comes out every morning at six to feed his hens. He told me that yesterday, just after six, he saw a clergyman walk up the path and disappear into the church. He thought nothing of it — after all, you'd expect to see a clergyman going into a church — but he did think it was very early for any kind of service, and in any case, he said, you'd expect to see "Mrs Vicar" going in there, not some stranger.'

'Did he say whether this clergyman was carrying a bag of some sort?'

'Yes, sir. He noticed it particularly because it was a bright red and yellow plastic bag, which made such a contrast to the man, who was dressed all in black.'

I began to form a theory involving that latter-day Witchfinder General, Julian Stringer, but held my peace.

At that point the Reverend Stacey returned to the church to tell us that the bishop and the archdeacon had just arrived. In a moment they had joined us in the church.

Bishop Poindexter is a cadaverous sort of man, with a skull-like head. He looks as though he's on the brink of death. He is, in fact, in perfect health, and very active in his diocese. I know him quite well, and he shook hands with me, but the archdeacon I had never seen before. He was an alert, solemn-looking man in his fifties, with thinning grey hair. He wore round gold-rimmed glasses. He was very new to the diocese, his predecessor having died in office.

French gave the two clerics a brief account of his investigation, mentioning in particular the appearance of an unidentified clergyman on the morning of the baptism, and the fact that someone — not the vicar — had sprinkled holy water on the pews. It was then that I put in my word.

'The former patron of the living, Colonel Calderdale, was visited by a strange clergyman the other day,' I said. 'I saw him myself, a man called the Reverend Julian Stringer. He was dead set against women priests, and called them by some fancy name — energumens, I think it was.'

I saw the look of understanding that passed between the bishop and the archdeacon.

'Yes, we know all about his activities,' said the bishop. 'The Reverend Julian Stringer is currently under interdict for causing public disturbances at services conducted by women clergy. He runs a society called the Warriors of Christ. Using holy water to cleanse a church "polluted" by a female vicar is one of his trademarks.'

I thought the bishop was too quick to assume that Stringer was the culprit. The archdeacon was more circumspect.

'It may be Julian Stringer,' he said, 'but we've no absolute proof that it is, Bishop. But what about the greater outrage? The filling of the font basin with pig's blood? I believe Stringer is unhinged, but would he stoop to such a blasphemy?' He shook his head. 'Don't you have a set of pagans around here, Doctor? Surely pig's blood is more their kind of thing?'

'I'm afraid the Master of the Goat Herd and his little group have alibis for the night in question,' Inspector French said smoothly. 'They were at some overnight retreat in the Cotswolds. They were awake all night, together, so that rather rules them out for this.'

The archdeacon appeared disappointed at this news, and I recognised a fellow gossip in that moment.

'We know for a fact that it was pig's blood, do we, Inspector?' he asked.

'Yes, sir. News of the outrage spread fast yesterday, and several people in the village wondered whether it was pig's blood that had been used. This is a rural parish, sir, and people know about things like that. Anyway, when I got here this morning I was met by the police constable from Newton Ferrars, who told me that a local farmer had noticed that someone had tampered with his supply of pig's blood, which he keeps in chromium-plated vats in one of his barns. The lid on one of those vats had not been put back properly, and there was blood splashed on the floor of the barn.'

'What does he want pig's blood for?' asked the bishop.

'To make black puddings, which he sells to local butchers and the public,' I said.

'So what it amounts to, gentlemen,' said DI French, 'is this. A clergyman of some sort obtained pig's blood and a bottle of holy water — he may have made that himself — and then came into this church to make his point about the Reverend Stacey. He may be mentally unstable, or just plain wicked, but we're going after him now, and we'll bring him to book. Pig's blood . . . This has all the hallmarks of a hate crime.'

I called on Stacey later in the day. She and Melanie were talking quietly together in the vicarage kitchen over mugs of tea. I must confess that I was hardly surprised when she told me that the bishop wanted her to take a sabbatical — a sort of clerical holiday away from the stresses of life at Holy Trinity.

'He wants me to go for a fortnight, doesn't he, Melanie? Old Canon Harper has very kindly agreed to come back for that time. It's a terrible setback to my career, but I can see the wisdom of it, and I'm prepared to be ruled by the bishop in the matter.'

'Bishop Poindexter thinks he knows who did it,' I said.

'Yes, and the police are going after him. I've had so many letters and phone calls of support, even from opponents.'

'Anything from Nigel?'

'No.' Stacey looked inexpressibly sad when she said this. I felt like going over to Rushbrooke House and knocking some sense and some humanity into Nigel's silly head.

'Where will you go?' I asked. It was at that moment that I realised I knew very little about Stacey Williams. Were her parents still living? Did she have siblings? She was already being defined solely by the outrages that had been perpetrated against her.

'I shall go to stay with the Sisters of Mary at Highfield Convent,' she replied. 'I've stayed with them before on retreat, and I know that I'll have peace and quiet there. They're an Anglican sisterhood.'

Melanie was not given much to speaking, but she had her say now.

'You should leave this place altogether, Vicar,' she said. 'They don't deserve you here, apart from people like Dr Miller. Tell the bishop that you're not coming back!'

'I wish it was as easy as that, Melanie,' she said, with a sad smile. 'There are procedures to go through . . . But yes, I think I've failed here. I seem to have stirred up a Devil's brew, though God knows it's none of my making.'

I saw her eyes fill with tears, and felt myself flushing with indignation. I made my excuses and left. Melanie followed me down the path as far as the gate.

'She trebled the congregation at her last church,' she said, clutching at my sleeve. 'She'd have done the same here, if the Devil hadn't decided to destroy her. I'm afraid, Dr Miller. I wish she'd leave *now*, this very day, before there's more harm done.'

Looking back at what happened next, her words seemed very much like a prophecy.

* * *

I am an early riser, and on Sundays I attend the seven o'clock Communion service at Holy Trinity. There are usually fifteen or twenty people present, and the service is spoken, so there's no need for my services as organist. At the Sung Eucharist I never leave the organ loft.

I remember that particular seven o'clock service for two reasons, which I'll explain in a minute. At the stroke of seven, the Reverend Stacey came out of the vestry and entered the sanctuary, accompanied by her server. It was impossible to believe that anything unpleasant had happened to her, she looked so serene and confident. As I explained earlier, we are — or rather were — a very Papalist church, so Stacey was using the Roman Missal. At Communion time we all trooped up the nave and knelt at the Communion rail, where Stacey then gave us the bread and wine of the Holy Eucharist. *The Body of Christ. Amen. The Blood of Christ. Amen.*

It was as I walked back to my seat in one of the threatened pews that I saw a dark figure sneaking along the south choir aisle. This was no congregant but an alien intruder. I caught up with the Reverend Julian Stringer before he could enter the vestry.

'Leave now, while you're able to do so,' I whispered. 'The police know about what you did here that Friday, and are after you. Go now, while you're still a free man.'

That's typical of me, I'm afraid. I'm too fond of giving people second chances.

He treated me to a hideous smile. His face was covered in sweat, and little beads of spit had formed at the corners of his mouth. It was grotesque to see a man of this type wearing the dog collar of a priest.

I saw then that he was holding a canvas shopping bag with a zip top. Something — or some things — were squirming about in the bag. I tore it from his hands, and he must have seen the rage in my eyes, because he turned on his heel, and ran back along the aisle. In a few moments he had left the church.

In a few minutes Stacey would finish the service, and would come back with the server. I hurried into the vestry and unlocked the door into the churchyard. Here, well away from the church, I unzipped the bag and freed the squeaking mice that Stringer had meant to release in the vestry. I realised then that Stringer was master of the pathetic but frightening gesture: pig's blood, scary mice. I also realised that he was dangerously insane. I didn't intend to tell Stacey about the incident before she went on holiday, but I would certainly let Detective Inspector French know.

I watched Stacey as she came out of the church and disappeared into the vestry with the server. Like me, she would have been fasting from Saturday night, and would go straight back to the vicarage where no doubt Melanie would have a decent cooked breakfast ready. I busied myself for a quarter of an hour in the organ loft, putting out the music for the eleven o'clock Sung Eucharist, and turned my mind to bacon and eggs.

And now for the second incident. As I made my way through the churchyard to the road, I glanced across at the vicarage, and saw Colonel Nigel Calderdale being admitted to the house by Melanie Grint. My unworthier self wondered whether he was about to perpetrate some outrage dreamt up by his friend Stringer, but then my better self hoped that here, at the eleventh hour, Nigel was going to offer Stacey some kind of apology for his appalling behaviour to her. I'm thankful to say that I was right about this, as I will explain later.

* * *

News that Stacey was going away for a 'rest' had spread through the parish, and the church was packed for the eleven o'clock Sung Eucharist. It was evident that the people of Rushbrooke Hill had decided to rally round their beleaguered vicar.

Stacey seemed to have regained some of her lost confidence, and conducted the service with an extra dose of panache. She spoke clearly, and had a trained voice, so that she sang her parts of the service very well. She was accompanied by two of the new servers. I glanced round the packed church, but Nigel wasn't there.

We came once more to the solemn moment of consecration, when the priest transforms the bread and wine into the Body and Blood of Christ. I watched Stacey performing the rite in the long mirror fixed above the organ console. As always, she lowered her voice as she performed the consecration, leaning forward over the altar.

'Take this, all of you, and eat of it, for this is my body, which will be given up for you.'

She raised the Host aloft, returned it to the altar table, and genuflected.

I thought to myself, *If you apologised to her, Nigel, then you should have come here this morning to seal your repentance.*

She consecrated the wine, and raised the chalice aloft, before returning it to the altar table, and genuflecting. She continued with the rite, and I watched her in the mirror as she showed the Host to the people, with the words: 'Behold the Lamb of God,' to which we replied, 'Lord I am not worthy.'

I watched as she made her own Communion, as always with her back to the people, bending low over the altar, as she ate her fragment of the Host. Then I saw her raise the chalice, and put it to her lips.

She gave a very brief choking cry, and the chalice fell from her hand on to the altar steps. Stacey landed like a rag doll on the sanctuary floor. The two servers began to scream. I clattered down the stairs from the organ loft and ran into the sanctuary. Too late, to my great grief. Stacey Williams was dead.

4. JOHN MILLER'S NARRATIVE:
AFTERMATH OF MURDER

'DEVIL'S WORK!' screamed the *Mirror*'s front page, along-side a picture of the church. It rather grabbed my attention as I stopped at the village newsagent's for a box of paper clips a few days after the murder. It was St George's Day, but our church was closed, and I didn't fancy travelling further afield to another church that day. It was also Shakespeare's birth-day, and I recalled those words from *Macbeth*: 'It will have blood; they say, blood will have blood.'

I cast my eye over an interview with 'a respected psy-chic', who claimed to have forecast Stacey's murder a week before it happened, though his spirit guide had told him to keep silent until now. The actual reportage was very sober and accurate. I looked at the array of other newspapers on the counter to see what the world at large thought of our murder. There was nothing in *The Sun*, which was preoccupied with the latest footballer's wife scandal. 'Shona vows: I will tell all' was the headline of the day. Stacey's murder made page three of *The Times*, where it was given a half-column of deadpan reporting without any personal comment. *The Daily Telegraph* also had it on page three, but with a photograph of the church, which looked as though it had been taken fifty years ago — what I believe is called a 'stock image' in the trade. 'Villagers appalled at murder of vicar' was the headline, and there was also a letter from someone in Lechlade bemoaning the decline in respect for religion in modern times.

I looked at the owner of the shop, who was busy polishing a spade.

'What do you think, Harry?' I asked.

'It's a damn shame. She was a nice lady, even if she was a bit bossy. Mind you, we both know who did it, don't we, Doctor?'

I was all ears. What did Harry Thompson and I know that nobody else did?

'Well, er . . .'

'It was those bloody heathens out at Mosspit Lane. The Goat Herds, or whatever they call themselves. They live together in that old house, indulging in pagan frolics, so I'm told, and the man who runs them is called the Master Goat, or something. Disgusting. One of the first things that the vicar did was to call on the Master Goat and tell him that his days were numbered. He didn't like that. You mark my words, it'll come out as it was them that did it in the end.'

I don't usually take much notice of Harry's opinions on social matters, but I must confess that I was very thoughtful as I walked home that morning.

* * *

Towards the end of that week, my old friend and bridge partner DI French came up from Oldminster to spend the day with me. He came with the conviction that the Reverend Julian Stringer had committed the murder for some deranged reason of his own.

Not unnaturally, he asked the obvious question.

'How could he have done it?'

It was rhetorical, of course: DI French knew quite well that I had no answer. The immediate autopsy on Stacey Williams showed that she had been poisoned with cyanide.

The smell of peaches arising from the carpet in the church had already told me that she had been poisoned by cyanide introduced into the chalice. By imbibing that lethal potion, she had died immediately.

'It comes in different forms,' he said. 'Cyanide, I mean. If you are what I'd call a systematic poisoner, you'd use it in minute quantities, so that your victim would suffer headaches, dizziness, a fast heartbeat — some of the symptoms of cardiac disorder — you know the kind of thing I mean, John. You've attended quite a few people with heart disease. In the end, your victim would suffer cardiac arrest, and their doctor would almost certainly give you a death certificate.'

'I know that it's very difficult to detect,' I said. 'At least, when administered in the way you've described. But surely that didn't apply to Stacey Williams?'

'No, decidedly not. She was given a lethal dose, and died immediately. Cyanide comes in different forms. There are a number of salts, but in Stacey's case the autopsy revealed that she had been given the liquid form of cyanide, usually known as hydrocyanic acid, or prussic acid.

'It makes you wonder, though, where he got it from. You can be killed by inhaling it if you're caught in a house fire, and it's used in insecticides of various types, and in the manufacture of plastics, among other things.

'But the cyanide that killed Stacey was in the form of prussic acid, a colourless liquid which had been added to the red wine in the chalice—'

'Not quite that,' I said. 'There would have been nothing in the chalice until Stacey poured a quantity of wine into it during the course of the service. No, the wine would have been prepared in a glass cruet in the vestry, before the service, together with a cruet containing water, placed on a tray, and then taken into the chancel by one of the servers. It would be placed on what is called a credence table, to the right of the altar. At the offertory, the server would have given Stacey the cruet of wine, and she would have poured this into the chalice. Then she would add a small quantity of water. You'll appreciate that I've watched this being done in reverse in the mirror over the organ console.'

'So the prussic acid would have been added to the cruet of wine in the vestry,' said DI French. 'He could have had it in a screw-top bottle in his pocket. All he would have to do was drink some of the wine from the cruet, and add his deadly poison to what remained. Incidentally, I thought there was always an offertory procession, with the bread and wine being brought up the aisle from the back of the church? That's what they do at the cathedral.'

'Stacey didn't think it was necessary,' I said. 'And she didn't like all the hand-shaking that goes on in some churches, so we didn't have that, either.'

'She was a lady of decided opinions,' offered DI French.

'She was, and she had a stubborn way about her that ensured her wishes were granted.'

'Are you quite sure that you didn't see this Reverend Stringer coming out of the vestry?'

'Yes, quite sure. He was sneaking down the south aisle towards the vestry door, carrying his disgusting bag of scary mice.'

'He might have been in the vestry earlier,' said French. 'I think he's one of those men who can hover and hide.'

I had to admit that this was a possibility.

'Who would have poured the wine from the bottle into the cruet? One of those two young girls?'

'No, Melanie would have done that. She's the sacristan, looking after the vestments, et cetera. She knows all about that kind of thing.'

'The press have gone to town over this,' said French, 'and I don't blame them. All the nationals covered the story, and apparently questions are to be asked in the House.' He chuckled. 'Much good that'll do!

'Now, we've initiated a search for this Reverend Julian Stringer. He lived in a flat in Chichester, where he moved after the Bishop of Oldminster put him under interdiction. Before that, he'd lived in Oldminster, in one of the apartments on Riverside. His cleaner hasn't seen him for days. He's gone to earth somewhere, but we'll find him.'

'Melanie Grint has taken this very badly,' I said. 'She was frantic at first, and I was afraid that she'd lose her mind. I gave her some stuff to calm her nerves, but I don't think she'll ever be the same.'

'But she's still here?'

'Oh, yes, she's still here. She's recovered enough to get in touch with Stacey's parents — I knew nothing about her private life, and wasn't aware that she had any parents.'

'Most people do.'

'Yes, but somehow Stacey Williams gave the impression that she was someone without family ties.'

'This Melanie Grint — do you think you could intro-duce me to her? She was briefly interviewed by PC Gaunt on that fatal Sunday, but I've never met her myself.'

I picked up the phone, and dialled Rushbrooke Vicarage.

* * *

It was a shock to see that a couple of packing cases had still not been opened. Poor Stacey had not lived long enough to settle down fully as vicar of Rushbrooke Hill.

Melanie had provided us with tea and biscuits, and DI French and I sat on one of the comfortable settees, listening to her account of what had happened on that fatal Sunday morning.

'The early Mass went off without a hitch,' she said. 'A nice, quiet service, Stacey said — well, you were there, Doctor, and can vouch for what I say. The vicar came back for breakfast, and then went into her study to read through the notes for her sermon, which she was due to deliver at the Sung Eucharist.'

Melanie still looked ill, and while she was speaking I was thinking about some further treatments. I was afraid that she could easily subside into a severe endogenous depres-sion. Her voice was flat, but her eyes burnt with some kind of unfathomable light. God knows what she was thinking about.

'I went across to the vestry at ten thirty, and prepared the cruets. Linda and Mary were already there, changing into cassock and surplice. They're the two servers who were on duty that day. Linda's thirteen, and Mary's eleven. Their mothers have said that they must not attend Holy Trinity anymore. Those poor children . . .'

She burst into tears, and held her face in her hands.

'They — they were there in the sanctuary when it happened,' she continued through her tears. 'Can you imagine it? They're only little girls . . .'

While she was talking, I saw that Paul French was looking around the room, and I knew that he was making a mental catalogue of its contents. He told me once that you could learn a lot about a victim or a perpetrator by examining how they lived.

'Let us return to your account of what happened in the vestry,' said DI French. 'You said that Linda and Mary were there.'

'Yes. I took the bottle of altar wine from the cupboard—'

'Excuse me, but was the cupboard locked? Did you open it with a key?'

Melanie Grint blushed with what looked like vexation.

'It's usually locked, and I have the key here, on my chain, but it wasn't locked that morning. The last time I was in that cupboard, someone distracted me, and I forgot to lock the cupboard door. But then, you don't expect a homicidal maniac to come skulking round a village church!'

'Quite,' said DI French drily. 'Now, this bottle of wine — can you describe it to me?'

'It's just a bottle of Jackson's Best Red Altar Wine. You'll find it in hundreds of church vestries. Their bottles have a screw top, not a cork. I filled one glass cruet with wine and the other with water, just like I always do. One of the servers took them through into the sanctuary. And by some devilish trick, that wine was somehow contaminated with poison, and poor Stacey died!'

'This bottle of wine — did anything seem odd about it?' asked French.

'Odd? No, it was just . . . Well, there *was* something, now I come to think of it. I found it quite difficult to unscrew the lid. It was very tight, and I had to grasp it with a towel to get it open.'

I saw that DI French's eyes were shining. I wondered what was making him so happy.

'It was all that Colonel Calderdale's fault,' said Melanie. 'He started all this by refusing to accept Stacey as vicar. How dare he! He came here that morning. His conscience must have been troubling him. And there he was, here, in the vicarage, as stiff and unsmiling as ever, to say that he regretted all the terrible things that had happened, and wanted to assure us that he had nothing to do with any of the vile persecutions that had been carried out against the vicar.'

'And what did the Reverend Stacey say to that?'

'I never let him get near her! I told him that I'd tell her what he'd said, and he had to be content with that. I *did* tell her, and she just gave that sad smile of hers and said, "It's a bit late in the day for that, Mel." It was, too! Within the hour she was dead.'

DI French glanced at me. It was time to go.

'Stacey's parents will be here tomorrow,' said Melanie Grint. 'I've spoken to them on the phone, and they're going to take her body back to London for burial. The sooner she's out of this cursed place the better!'

'So what do you think?' I asked, when we were back in the road. 'I saw you glancing round, doing an inventory of the room. What did you find?'

'It was what I didn't find that interested me,' he said. 'There were no family photographs, no pictures of herself in academic or clerical garb. I just wondered, that's all.'

'And what was all that about the wine bottle?'

'First, it's apparently readily available — it's the kind of thing that any clergyman could get his hands on. And second, it was almost too tight for Miss Grint to open. I just imagined our Mr Stringer coming here with his own doctored bottle of the identical wine, hoping that the cupboard was unlocked, and then making a substitution. I'm just supposing that a man's screwing of the bottle top would be stronger than a woman's, which is why Melanie had some trouble in unscrewing it.'

'Amazing, my dear Holmes!'

'On the contrary, Watson, quite elementary. Poor Melanie unwittingly poisoned her employer because that man had succeeded in substituting his own poisoned bottle for the perfectly innocent one. We must run this killer to earth before he decides to take out another vicar!'

* * *

I never saw Stacey's parents, though they arrived soon after the murder and, Melanie told me, had arranged for her body to be taken to London for the funeral. Two large furniture vans appeared at the vicarage. Meanwhile, Bishop Poindexter had ordered the closure of Holy Trinity and all its buildings, and our congregation had been offered the hospitality of the local Methodist church hall as a place of worship until our church had been exorcised and reconsecrated. Old Canon Harper and what you might call a 'faithful remnant' fitted out the Methodist church hall as a passable place of Anglican worship, and the congregation began to drift back. The parish church remained locked, forlorn and profaned.

Melanie Grint simply left one day without informing any of us. I was hardly surprised. In a spirit of nosiness I made enquiries at the bus depot, and learnt that she had caught a bus to Oldminster, and had been dropped off at the train station. Perhaps she had caught a train there to London — I'd gathered from various things she'd said that, like Stacey, she was a Londoner. I had formed a rather grudging liking for her, and was sorry that she had left without seeing me.

We held a sort of unofficial PCC meeting in Rushbrooke House, and discussed parish affairs, including the tiresome business of yet another interregnum. Alan Shirtcliffe made a speech about the need for new beginnings, and the heeding of various lessons to be learnt from the recent demonic infestation. Everybody agreed that this was the right spirit, and then it was time for a much chastened Nigel Calderdale to have his say.

'If we're to start all over,' he said, 'I'd like to resume my patronage of the living, if that's all right with you, Alan. And this time, I will faithfully endorse whatever decisions the PCC takes. I'll become an enabler rather than a thorn in the flesh. Are you content to let me resume the patronage?'

Alan, bless him, was only too eager to fall in with Nigel's suggestion.

As we left the meeting I managed to get Nigel to myself.

'Nigel,' I said, 'does this mean that you've changed your mind about the validity of women priests?'

'Certainly not,' he replied. 'My views on that will never change, and I think that Mr Stringer is being maligned before there's any kind of proof that he was involved in that dreadful affair. But in future, as patron, I will accept whoever the committee chooses without any fuss. I've promised to do that, and I intend to keep my word.'

And so life went on as it always had in Rushbrooke Hill. It is now almost a month since Stacey was killed. There are fields to tend, the shops to visit, and the many tasks and preoccupations typical of a rural village. Nigel Calderdale came to see me about sleeplessness, and I prescribed a mild sedative. Even the Chief Goat, clad in his ridiculous robes, came to consult me, convinced that he had a stomach ulcer. He hadn't, and I prescribed a bottle of magnesium trisilicate. I was tempted to ask him if he'd tried using his magical powers to treat his tummy ache, but I held my peace.

5. THE SAXON WOOD POISONING

'You *will* catch him, won't you, Paul?' asked Moira French as she and her husband sat at breakfast.

'Don't worry, we'll catch him.' DI French was silent for a while as he finished eating his scrambled egg on toast. 'I'm handing the next phase of the investigation to Glyn Edwards as I've other fish to fry this month. Is there any more tea in that pot?'

'I think it's disgraceful,' said Moira. 'What kind of man would murder a vicar by poisoning the wine in the chalice? And a clergyman, too! He ought to be defrocked before he's locked up for life.'

'Well, you see—'

'The whole country's talking about it, while you just sit there eating breakfast! I don't know what's happening to Oldshire. An innocent vicar murdered in her own church! Who's going to be next? The bishop? I'm already seeing pieces in the paper about young men feeling threatened by equality — as if that's some kind of excuse for killing a woman who was just doing her job. I suppose when you *do* catch him — and I have my doubts about that — some psychiatrist will say that murdering the Reverend Stacey Williams was "a cry for help". I've no time for it.'

'This very morning,' said Moira's husband, 'Detective Sergeant Glyn Edwards is going to visit Bishop Poindexter to find out all he can about the Reverend Julian Stringer. After that, he will go out looking for him. You mark my words, Moira, Glyn will soon come up with the goods. Is that the time? I must get down to Jubilee House. Superintendent Philpot wants to see me at nine.'

* * *

The cathedral city of Oldminster is a thriving market town, the county seat of Oldshire. It lies well to the north of its great rival, Chichester. Oldminster is a successful blend of the ancient and modern, with its famous Regency squares and terraces in what is known as Old Town, in the shadow of the great cathedral church of St Peter, which overlooks Cathedral Green. There is a bustling town centre, with shops of all kinds, including branches of M&S, Next and other very welcome retail outlets. On the far side of the town, in a suburb called Riverside, is a large and well-patronised branch of Sainsbury's.

In its own walled garden to the south of Oldminster Cathedral stands the bishop's palace, a long, low, pebble-dash building of two storeys, completed in 1907 after the old palace had burnt down in the 1890s. Here lives the widowed Bishop, the Right Reverend Gabriel Poindexter, a tall, lean, corpse-pale man with a very fine bald head. He is sixty-three, broad church in outlook, and with a guarded tolerance for other people's views on the nature of the Church.

The bishop knew Detective Sergeant Edwards through his connection with the murder of Bridget Messiter, and was happy to invite him to sit in one of the more comfortable chairs in his study overlooking the palace lawn.

'This is a terrible business, Sergeant Edwards,' he said. 'I don't know how far I'm to blame, but I confess that I have tolerated that man in my diocese because he and I were trained together. We were ordained on the same day, as it happens, and by the same bishop.'

Sergeant Edwards was looking better, fuller in the face, and less hangdog than he had been in the past. He had always seemed older than his years, but he had had many burdens to bear during his wife's long bout of mental illness. All that, thank God, was behind him, now.

'I've brought a dossier here from the archives,' said the bishop. 'It will tell you all that you'll want to know about Julian Stringer's career. He's not an Anglo-Catholic, you know, he's an old-fashioned evangelical, and when the question of women's ordination was first mooted, he became a very strident opponent. He joined various pressure groups in the Synod, some quite laudable, others decidedly sinister, and when the first woman bishop was consecrated in England, he founded the Warriors of Christ.'

'I know about them, Bishop,' said Glyn Edwards. 'The name sounds very grand, but in fact there are only seven members, and they meet once a month in a rented room above a fish and chip shop behind the Beaver Street bus depot. As far as I know, they're a native product of Oldminster. There are similar groups in London and elsewhere, but none of them are as vicious as this little lot. Those other groups' usual tactics are to bray out infantile slogans at meetings, and wave little homemade placards in the air.'

The bishop smiled in spite of himself. Glyn Edwards had the ability to cut people and organisations down to size. But he was only partly right about the Warriors.

'They may be few in numbers, Sergeant, but they have the capacity to make people's lives very unpleasant. It only takes one or two to disrupt an ordination, but the effect on the victim can be profound. The loss of self-worth can last a lifetime. I've no powers to act against the lay members, unfortunately. I was talking to Monsignor Benson the other day, and he asked me why I didn't just excommunicate them. I told him that we didn't have that option in the Church of England, and he treated me to one of his special smirks, which I took in good part.

'But there was one way in which I *could* act against Julian Stringer, and I put him under an interdict, which is one step on the way to laicisation.'

'Kicking him out.'

'Precisely. But I think it's only made him worse. That business at Rushbrooke Hill — pig's blood in the font, an attempt to release mice into the vestry, and then, finally, most blasphemous murder. I fear his mind has turned.'

'Don't try to get him off the hook, Bishop,' said Glyn Edwards. 'With all due respect, I've known you to try bringing insanity as a defence of one of your erring colleagues before. Let's catch him first, and then the law can decide on the state of his mind, and act accordingly.'

Glyn thought, *Has he taken offence? No, he and I have been bound up with some vile crimes, the solution of what has formed a link of trust between us.* But the bishop had just said something that sent an alarm bell ringing in his mind. What was it? No, it had gone.

'Does he still have a parish?'

'Oh, no, Sergeant, before now I forbade him to officiate he had gone into the wilderness. He resigned his last parish some years ago, as I recall. Since then, he's been a kind of freelance preacher and troublemaker.'

Bishop Poindexter had got up from his desk, and was standing at the window. Presently he returned to his seat, and uttered a mournful sigh.

'Sergeant,' he said, 'I'm going to tell you something now that I don't want spread abroad to all and sundry. Obviously, you can tell Paul French — he'll have to know. When Julian Stringer was serving his first curacy at a church in Berkshire, he formed an attachment to a young lady in the church choir, and by all accounts a bit of a romance blossomed. But then, I don't know why, the young lady abruptly ended the relationship. Soon after, she announced her engagement to a young man in the congregation.'

'Perhaps she discovered something about his character that sent up warning signs,' said Glyn. 'In any case, it was her privilege to break off the relationship, if that's what she wanted.'

'But there was more than that,' said the bishop. 'A couple of weeks after the engagement, there was a hotpot supper held in the church hall, and both the young lady and her fiancé were taken violently ill. Nobody else was affected. Mercifully they both recovered, but a doctor present — not the local doctor — described their symptoms as those of arsenical poisoning. Nothing was ever proved, but rumours persisted. Stringer accepted another curacy in a different town soon afterwards.'

'And what do you deduce from that, Bishop?'

'I'm suggesting that Stringer's misogyny — for that's what it is — stemmed from that early rebuttal. Some men can be vengeful in that way. He never married.'

'Plenty of us are rejected and manage to avoid dedicating our lives to hate crimes,' Glyn said lightly. 'It's just as likely that he was already a misogynist and when the young lady realised, she chose someone more suitable.'

'Ah, well, it may be as you say. The upshot was that he was an embarrassment I could do little about. Please take this file. It will tell you all you want to know about Stringer's clerical career. Perhaps you'll find more clues to his motives or his whereabouts than I have been able to discern.'

'And you can't suggest where he might be now, Bishop?'

'No. He could be anywhere. If you look in that dossier you'll see that both his parents are dead, and he had no siblings. I wish you well in your quest, Sergeant Edwards.'

* * *

In the room above the chip shop Glyn Edwards found two earnest men and one tearful woman sitting at a trestle table. The room was illuminated by a single light bulb, and a table near the window held the remnants of a couple of takeaways. The Warriors of Christ were busy making banners to unfurl at some unfortunate woman's ordination. One of the Warriors, an alarmingly respectable-looking man in an expensive suit, tackled Edwards head on. He had an educated, rather hectoring voice, which he used perhaps to good effect when addressing his own followers or haranguing his opponents.

'No, Sergeant, I don't know where Julian Stringer is, and if I did I wouldn't tell you. Free speech is under threat in this country, and so is freedom of religion. Scripture tells us that the Prince of this World is come, and Scripture never errs. The Devil goeth about, seeking whom he may devour. Well, some of us, both Anglo-Catholic and Evangelical, are willing in these latter days to stand up to him. We may be few, but remember Our Lord's words: "When two or three are gathered together in My name, there am I in the midst of them".'

The well-dressed man sat down. He looked quite pleased with himself. The other man, thin-faced and with restless eyes, took over. His voice was quieter, more wheedling, as though his tactic was to persuade rather than bully.

'Do you not believe that the Scriptures are the Word of God, Sergeant? Or have you decided that God doesn't matter anymore in our modern society? "Be not deceived: God is not mocked. For whatsoever a man soweth, that also shall he reap".'

'Galatians six, verse seven,' said the man in the expensive suit. The tearful woman bent closer over her work, and the thin-faced man continued to address Glyn Edwards.

'In opposing the so-called "ordination" of women, Sergeant, we are simply obeying the plain words of Scripture, which is God's Word written. So let me quote you some words from one Corinthians fourteen, verses thirty-three to thirty-five: "As in all the congregations of the Lord's people, women should remain silent in the churches. They are not allowed to speak, but must be in submission, as the law says. If they want to inquire about something, they should ask their own husbands at home; for it is disgraceful for a woman to speak in the church".'

'And you don't know where Julian Stringer is to be found?'

'I don't,' said the well-dressed man. 'He has fled from the inevitable persecution. You see, he has been framed, to use a vulgar word. Evidence was planted against him, and people like you believed that evidence. So he knows that there is no justice for him in this country.'

The man wiped a fleck of spittle from his mouth and seemed to master himself with the action.

'You don't believe me, do you?' he continued. 'I'm talking about that business at Rushbrooke Hill that was in all the papers. Do you seriously think that an ordained clergyman would profane a font by filling it with pig's blood? And more than that, do you think he would profane God's altar poisoning the wine at Holy Communion? These are things the godless press would have you believe. We are Warriors of Christ, Sergeant, not assassins.'

'And now,' said the thin-faced man, 'I expect you'll want to take down our names and addresses. Or are you going to arrest us? Oh, don't cry, Gladys, there's a dear.'

'Your religious beliefs are your own concern', said Glyn Edwards, 'but as far as I know, you've committed no crime, and I have no right to demand your names and addresses. All I wanted to do was to ask you whether you knew where Julian Stringer was. I take note of what you said about him, but have you considered that he may be in danger? He will be very vulnerable at this moment. If, as you suggest, he has committed no crime, then he has nothing to fear from talking to the police.'

The well-dressed man seemed to relax, and Glyn saw that he was being viewed with something like respect.

'No, we've nothing to hide, Sergeant. My name is Joseph Peterson. This man with me is Reginald Vholes, and that lady is Gladys Timms, Mr Vholes's cousin.' He added in slightly embarrassed tones, 'None of us had anything to do with the outrages at Rushbrooke Hill. We are all at you service.'

* * *

Glyn Edwards read through the dossier that Bishop Poindexter had given him, and found there the record of Julian Stringer's first curacy. He had arrived in 1980 at the village of Saxon Wood, a few miles north of Reading. He had been appointed to assist the Reverend Canmore Ballantyne at St Mary's church. He had stayed only a year, moving in 1981 to a second curacy in the diocese of Chichester. The dossier gave full details of all his subsequent appointments until his abandoning the ministry in 2015, and his forced resignation on the orders of Bishop Poindexter, after which he had drifted into a wilderness of his own making. But it was that first curacy that interested DS Edwards: that rumour of poisoning at a church event had some echoes in recent events. Perhaps it could be the key to Stacey Williams's death.

There were good, fast trains to Reading from Oldminster, and a regular bus service from there to Saxon Wood. Glyn decided to make the excursion the next day. The bus from Reading deposited him at the village cross in Saxon Wood, where he found an old-fashioned pub, the Saxon Arms, that provided him with a pint of beer and a plate of sandwiches. The place was empty, and the landlord seemed happy to have a bit of company. He joined Glyn at his table in the bar window, hovering expectantly.

'A police detective? That's very interesting. We used to have a police station here, but that's gone now, together with the post office. We're little more than a suburb of Reading, now. I blame this government . . .'

Glyn listened to the landlord's mournful recollections of life in the old days. He couldn't have been more than thirty, but he talked like an old man.

'Well, Mr Atwell, I'm afraid there are changes all around these days.'

'How did you know my name?'

'It's written over your door: "Leslie Atwell, licensed to sell intoxicating liquor". I've come here this morning to have a word with the vicar.'

'There's no vicar here now,' said Mr Atwell with gloomy relish. 'After Canmore Ballantyne died, he was never replaced. There's an old clergyman who comes out here once a month. He had three parishes to run. So you're here on church business?'

'As a matter of fact, Mr Atwell, I'm looking into an old village scandal dating back to the 1980s. Something to do with a young couple who were taken ill, and people thought they might have been poisoned.'

'Fancy you knowing about that! Yes, it was getting on for forty years ago. I wasn't born then, but my pa told me all about it. A nine days' wonder, it was. People thought the curate had done it, on account of the girl he fancied chucking him, and going after another young man. But that wasn't true, so my pa said.'

'What happened to them?'

'What happened to who?'

'The young couple that were taken ill.'

'Oh, they married, right enough, and he got work in a factory up in the north. And the curate moved on to a new job somewhere else.'

'Thank you very much, Mr Atwell,' said Glyn. 'It's been nice talking to you.'

'Why don't you go and talk to old Dr Thorpe? He'll tell you all about it. He ran the village practice until it got shut down. Now, we're supposed to travel miles to see a doctor in a big medical centre in Reading. Go and see Dr Thorpe. He lives in a cottage on the other side of the green.'

Dr Thorpe proved to be a genial man in his seventies, with bright eyes and an enquiring mind. His cottage was crammed with period oak furniture, and there were many horse brasses adorning the brick chimney piece.

'I don't get many visitors, Sergeant,' he said, 'so a police officer is an interesting curiosity. You tell me that Leslie Atwell sent you here. So what's it all about?'

'I'm making enquiries into an incident that occurred here nearly forty years ago, Doctor. A young couple who became ill at a hotpot supper. There was some talk of jealousy on the part of the curate at the local church—'

'Yes, I remember it well. I was already in practice then, and was called in when it happened. There was another doctor there, a visitor, who loudly declared that it was arsenical poisoning before now the victims had been properly examined. That's when the gossiping started.

'We had our own vicar then, and a curate, too. It was a nice, old-fashioned evangelical church, and a lot of people went to it. Mr Canmore Ballantyne was the vicar — a real gentleman of the old school — and Mr Julian Stringer was the new curate. It was his first curacy.'

'And he fell in love with a girl in the parish?'

'Well, yes, there was a nice little friendship of sorts, and I think Mr Stringer was convinced that she would marry him. But she didn't. They were never formally engaged, and she fell for someone else. They married a year later, and went off north somewhere.'

'And people began to talk—'

'Yes, they did. There was a lot of small-minded, ignorant gossip, and people pointed the finger at poor Julian Stringer. It was outrageous! Poisoned, people said. Poisoned! It was gastroenteritis. I gave them both an emetic to make them bring up whatever still remained in their stomachs, and tested the contents. I found some partly digested remains of shellfish, and they told me that they'd eaten shellfish at a market stall in Reading earlier that day. *That*, Sergeant, was what made them so very ill. There were positive traces of dinoflagellate algae, mercifully in only a small quantity. They both made quick and full recoveries, and as I told you they left the village the next year, and never came back.

'But poor Julian Stringer — well, people avoided him, and many churchgoers wouldn't come to church when he was officiating. He stuck it for a while, and then moved on elsewhere. But I think that business of the hotpot supper blighted the rest of his career.'

'He's in great trouble now, Doctor, under suspicion of having poisoned a vicar with cyanide. He's gone to ground. He's long been inhibited from talking services, and there are many people who think that he's become unhinged.'

'Yes, I've read something about it in the papers, and I'm more sorry than I can say. But I don't believe a word of what they're saying about him in the papers. He was crucified here in Saxon Wood by so-called public opinion, and I expect the same thing's happening to him in Oldminster now. He may not be a very pleasant man, Sergeant, but I doubt very much that he's a cold-blooded killer. Very few clergymen are.'

* * *

Later that afternoon, Sergeant Edwards, back at Jubilee House, the county police headquarters, received a letter that had been handed in to the desk sergeant.

Dear Mr Edwards, I don't think I can endure much more of this. I'm sick of persecuting other women just because I don't believe in their claims. Please don't tell the others that I told you this, because they were telling the truth when they said they didn't know. Julian Stringer is hiding in Holy Cross Abbey at West Deering. Yours truly, Gladys Timms.

Glyn muttered vehemently to himself. He'd spent the whole morning driving about doing good police work only to find the solution had been waiting for him on his desk all along. With a sigh, he snatched up his car keys, still not sure if he was pleased or annoyed.

6. SINNERS ANONYMOUS

Holy Cross Abbey was not as DS Edwards had envisioned it. It was not a romantic Gothic ruin, but a substantial Victorian house standing in a few acres of garden. He rang the bell, and the door was opened by a young man with a shaven head, dressed in the habit of a Franciscan friar. Somewhere in the house a bell was rung, perhaps summoning the monks to prayer.

The young man led DS Edwards along a musty passage, its walls adorned with rather alarming religious paintings, and knocked at the door at the far end. In a moment he found himself in the presence of the Abbot.

'Detective Sergeant Edwards? I am Abbot Richardson. Do sit down, please. Would you like a glass of sherry, or mustn't you drink on duty? What can I do for you?'

The Abbot was a very substantial man wearing a black cassock. Balding and double-chinned, he looked anything between fifty and sixty. His study was comfortably furnished, and reeked of vape fumes.

'You're well hidden away from the world here, sir,' said Glyn Edwards. 'I don't think I'd have spotted the place if I didn't already have the address.'

If the Abbot was curious about how Glyn had found the address, he didn't show it. 'We're an independent order of clergy,' he said. 'There are only eight of us here, including myself. West Deering is a nice, quiet village, more of a hamlet, really. We have our own beehives, and produce a very fine honey, which sells well. We have a thriving vegetable garden, and take our products regularly to the farmers' market. And so we get by. Are you sure you won't have a glass of sherry?'

Rather to his surprise, Glyn Edwards found himself consenting. There was something about this big man with the booming voice that appealed to him.

They sipped their sherry in silence for a while, and then the Abbot picked up an e-cigarette and inhaled deeply.

'*Mea culpa,*' he said, striking his breast. 'I know it's wrong, but it's my only vice. Well, maybe not my *only* vice . . . You've come about Julian Stringer, haven't you?'

The question took Glyn by surprise.

'Yes, Abbot,' he said. 'During the course of an investigation, I was told that he was here. I would like to see him, if that's possible.'

Abbot Richardson took another pull on his e-cigarette, then set it down in an empty ashtray.

'Everybody here is spiritually and mentally broken in some way, and I offer them spiritual healing in conjunction with a Jungian psychiatrist. Some are sent here by the Church. Others, like Julian Stringer, find their own way here. The quietude of an abbey, and the wearing of monastic habit for those who wish to, helps to anchor these men in a surrounding of stability. Not so much Franciscans or Benedictines as Sinners Anonymous.'

'Are they all clergymen?'

'Yes.'

'I'd very much value your opinion of the Reverend Julian Stringer's mental state.'

'Quite frankly, Sergeant, I think he needs to be confined for a time to a psychiatric hospital. Dr Weinreb agrees. He and I thought that in a week's time we'd start the process of moving him. He's very disturbed — his accounts of his actions lack coherence. He no longer seems able to distinguish between fact and fantasy.'

'I'd like to talk to him now, Abbot, if I may. He is the prime suspect in a murder investigation. I expect you know all about the trouble at Rushbrooke Hill?'

'Oh, yes — though I didn't realise he was a suspect. He isn't a murderer, as you'll see. He's told me all about his misdemeanours, though as I say he can't distinguish now between fact and fantasy. I believe some of the things he tells me; other things I take with a pinch of salt.'

'Allegations of various types have been made against him in the past, one at least of which is apparently without foundation, so I've not come here entirely prejudiced against him.'

'Come, you shall see him now. Have you any objection to my staying in the room?'

'None at all.' DS Edwards followed the Abbot along a carpeted corridor which opened out into a quiet enclave containing a suite of rooms, in one of which Julian Stringer was staying. The Abbot knocked briskly on the door, and they went in.

The Reverend Julian Stringer was sitting at a table piled high with books. He was reading the Bible, but half rose as they entered.

'Sit down, Julian,' said the Abbot. 'I've brought a visitor to see you. This is Detective Sergeant Edwards of the Oldshire Constabulary.'

'An officer of the law? Well, Mr Edwards, I must warn you that they will have domination for a while — the demons of the air — until the Lord decides to crush them under His feet. At that time you will come into your own. They shall burn in everlasting fire with their human helpers. None shall be spared.'

Stringer seemed to make a strong effort to concentrate on the business of the moment.

'Pleased to meet you, Sergeant,' he said. 'It was very clever of you to find me here. Or did someone betray me?'

Stringer looked as though he was on the border of insanity. His face twitched regularly, and his eyes seemed unable to focus properly.

After DI French had interviewed Dr John Miller and the housekeeper, Melanie Grint, he had suggested ways in which this unstable priest could have substituted his own poisoned bottle of wine for the harmless one kept in the vestry cupboard. 'When you finally track him down, Glyn,' he'd said, 'ask him about that. Tell him my theory, and see what his reaction is.' He would tackle Stringer about that, but not just yet.

'Mr Stringer,' he said, 'was it you who sprinkled the pews in Holy Trinity, Rushbrooke Hill, with holy water?'

'Yes, I told the Abbot that. I had a flask of holy water in my bag. After the abomination at the font, I wanted to cleanse the church of the evil spirits lurking there.'

'And you put the pig's blood in the font to vex the Reverend Miss Williams?'

'The blood in the font? How dare you suggest that! I used the holy water to cleanse the place after that dangerous energumen had profaned the font for the Devil's purposes.'

'You really think that *Reverend Williams* did that?'

Stringer's hand hovered around his mouth. He looked at the Abbot with something like fear.

'Or was it *me* who did that, Abbot? Did Satan seize me for a while as his unconscious instrument, and made me profane the font with pig's blood? No, it was *her*, the energumen, the woman possessed, who did it. I am the scourge of the Lord . . .'

Glyn Edwards suddenly recalled what Bishop Poindexter had said to him. *That business at Rushbrooke Hill — pig's blood in the font, an attempt to release mice in the vestry, and then finally, most blasphemous murder. I fear his mind has turned.* In a single sentence the bishop had coupled blasphemy and murder with the business of the mice, a coupling that made little sense to Glyn.

'Mr Stringer,' said Glyn, 'tell me about your attempt to release some mice into the vestry.'

Stringer giggled. It was a horrible sound, which chilled DS Edwards to the bone.

'Women are afraid of mice, aren't they? I thought I'd teach Miss Bossy Boots a lesson. I imagined her prancing into the vestry dressed up as a priest, and ending up screaming, standing on top of the vestment chest until someone rescued her!'

'A bit naughty, wasn't it?' said Glyn, forcing himself to smile.

'Yes, it was. A bit of a schoolboy prank, but the doctor stopped me from getting into the vestry, and I beat a hasty retreat!'

'And then later on that day, the Reverend Stacey Williams was murdered at the altar, having drunk from the poisoned chalice. You hated her, didn't you? Because you saw her as the instrument of Satan?'

'Yes. A most dangerous energumen, sent to destroy the Church from within. And she is not the only one. I know for a fact that there are others. I have seen them.'

'So maybe this is what you did, Mr Stringer. Correct me if I am wrong. Sometime before the Sung Eucharist, you came unseen into the vestry, bringing with you a bag containing a bottle of altar wine — the same brand as used at Holy Trinity, which is readily available. You had added a lethal quantity of hydrocyanic acid to your bottle, which you substituted for the bottle you took from the vestry cupboard, which had been carelessly left unlocked. That was all you had to do. Later, when you'd sneaked away, the sacristan came in, and poured some of the doctored wine into the cruet. Your energumen's fate was now sealed. At the holiest part of the Eucharist, she drank from the chalice, and died immediately.'

Julian Stringer had been rocking to and fro while Glyn was talking. Now he stopped, and stood up, standing still and expectant.

'Did I do that?' he whispered. 'Had I been once more possessed to do the Devil's work? Was I, all along, another instrument of Satan, along with those diabolical women? No! I don't believe it! I never went into the vestry that morning. In fact, to my recollection, I never at any time went into that vestry at all. Abbot, surely you know that I could never have done such a wicked thing?'

'Of course, of course,' said the Abbot. 'Try to put the whole business out of your mind. Dr Weinreb will be coming to chat with you soon. And then you must come to lunch as usual in the refectory. Why not lie down for a while?'

They left him, and returned to the Abbot's study.

'What do you think, Sergeant?' asked the Abbot, as soon as he had taken another draw from his e-cigarette.

'I'm beginning to think that he's not the man we're after. I haven't enough evidence to arrest him, and I'm going to leave him here with you. Did you know about his little romance when he was a young curate, a romance that turned sour?'

'Yes, he told me all about that.'

'Even in those days, Abbot, people misinterpreted his actions. The young woman chucked him and got engaged to someone else. When she and her fiancé fell ill, it was immediately assumed that Stringer had poisoned them. I have proof positive that he did nothing of the sort.'

'And his part in the business at Rushbrooke Hill?'

'The way it was told to me, people have coupled desecration and murder with the business of the mice in the bag. The three things didn't fit. I very sadly agree that Mr Stringer is not well, mentally speaking, but there's something about the way he laughed about those mice: silliness. He thought of it as a prank, almost. That's quite different to profaning the font, something he held in reverence. After the blood incident, he tried to cleanse the church by sprinkling holy water. He's mad, all right, but not raving.'

'So what you are saying—'

'What I am saying is, I don't believe he put that blood in the font. And I don't believe he poisoned the wine at that fatal Eucharist. Hydrocyanic acid was used. Where would Stringer have obtained such a lethal substance? You can't just buy it over the counter. I was partly persuaded of his innocence by something that one of his Warriors of Christ lackeys said to me the other day. I can recall his exact words. "Do you seriously think that an ordained clergyman would profane a font by filling it with pig's blood? And more than that, do you think that he would profane God's altar by adding poison to the wine at Holy Communion?" And the answer that I give you now is: No, I don't. I need to look elsewhere.'

* * *

Twelve miles out from Oldminster, and deep in the country-side, lay Staunton Old Hall, the residence of Lord Renfield. Frank Renfield had only recently recovered from a series of devastating blows that would have destroyed a lesser man, and with the help of his son-in-law the American millionaire Karl Langer, was enjoying a kind of renaissance at his newly acquired home, an ancient Tudor manor house.

'So how can I help you, Calderdale?' asked Frank Renfield. 'I've enjoyed seeing you again after all these years, and giving you lunch, but you've not told me what you *want*. If you're short of ready cash—'

'Good God, Frank,' Nigel Calderdale exclaimed in horror, 'it's nothing like that! No, it's — well, I think I did an innocent woman a great wrong, and I want to do something to put it right. I think I allowed myself to become obsessed with an idea, and that obsession changed me from a fairly decent person into a raving maniac.'

'You were always highly thought of in the regiment, Nigel.'

'Oh, yes, and they were good days. But the man I was then, a colonel, and for a while a field officer general staff, no less, morphed into a sort of country squire with the rights of patronage to a Church of England living. I enjoyed it all immensely, until — well, this is where I managed to re-create myself as a kind of swivel-eyed lunatic.'

Lord Renfield looked at his guest, and thought, *A couple of years ago I'd have told him to get a grip, and stop talking nonsense. But this last year has taught me a lot about mental anguish. If it hadn't been for my daughter Jessica, and my wonderful son-in-law Karl, I would have gone under.*

Aloud, he said, 'Come through into my library, Nigel. I've got some very special brandy there, and while we enjoy a glass or two, you can tell me your story, and then tell me what it is you want me to do.'

* * *

'And there it is, Frank, the whole wretched story.'

'I read about it in the papers,' said Lord Renfield, 'and knew that the murder of that poor lady took place on your patch, as it were. But I hadn't realised how deeply you were concerned in the matter. All those things you've told me — the picketing, the barracking, the refusal even to meet that lady when she was appointed to the parish — well, Nigel, I would not describe any of those things as the actions of a gentleman.'

He had the satisfaction of seeing his guest blush to the roots of his hair. He, Frank, was no angel, but he knew how to be a force for good when confronted with the likes of Colonel Nigel Calderdale.

'We'll say no more about that, Nigel — here, have another drink. But you hinted that you wanted me to do something for you. Out with it, man!'

'I haven't changed my views about female vicars,' he said, 'but I've been jolted by recent events into putting things in proportion, and I want to make amends if I can for my failure to protect that poor woman. I believe you know a firm of discreet private investigators in Oldminster, who might undertake a commission for me. You see, I think the police are going after the wrong man, and that the solution to the Reverend Stacey Williams's death lies somewhere in her past. I want someone who can delve into her early days, her life in other parishes, to see if there is anything there that could have contributed to her murder.'

'Hmm . . . So you've managed to throw off all that vicious nonsense about a woman possessed by the Devil? As you told it to me, it sounded like an awful lot of tosh.'

'Yes. I've even been to see Bishop Poindexter, and asked him to give me absolution, which he very kindly did. I want to make amends. If I'd kept my beliefs to myself and accepted that woman as vicar, I don't doubt that she'd still be alive today.'

'Well, you've come to the right place,' said Frank Renfield. 'I can write you an introduction to Greenspan & McArthur, who undertook some delicate enquiries for me with complete success. Noel Greenspan and Chloe McArthur are experienced investigators. They're not cheap, but if there's anything there for them to find, then they'll find it.'

* * *

The offices of Greenspan & McArthur were situated in Canal Street, an undistinguished, rundown thoroughfare in an unfashionable area of Oldminster beyond the train station. However, Nigel Calderdale was reassured when he had climbed the stairs from the street and found himself in a neat, modern office, neon-lit, with beige fitted carpet and walls painted a bland magnolia. A stout, ungainly man with the beginnings of a double chin rose from his chair to greet him.

'Colonel Calderdale? I am Noel Greenspan. I have Lord Renfield's letter here. How can I be of service?'

As he spoke, Greenspan indicated a smartly dressed woman at the next desk, who rose to shake Calderdale's hand. Her desk was neat where Greenspan's was cluttered, Calderdale noticed. 'This is my partner, Mrs Chloe McArthur,' said Greenspan. 'We are both at your service.'

Nigel Calderdale found himself blushing. He'd never had anything to do with people of this sort before, and didn't know where to begin. It was a bit like going to confession, not with a priest, but with an overweight man in a baggy suit, and a decidedly attractive lady.

'I've come to ask you to look into the earlier career of an Anglican vicar who was murdered in the church where I'm the patron. I'm convinced that the police are going about solving that murder in the wrong way, and that the answer lies hidden somewhere in that poor woman's past.'

Chloe McArthur treated him to a bewitching smile.

'That would be the Reverend Stacey Williams,' she said. 'Masters from Cambridge, Diploma in Theology from the University of London. She was born in 1974, and so was forty-five when she died. She was educated at a private girls' secondary school from 1985 to 1991. She was at Cambridge 1991 to 1994. Are we talking about the same person?'

'Yes. But how did you—'

'She was ordained deacon in 1997, and priest the following year. She then served two curacies, was vicar of a London parish for ten years, after which she went to a country parish, Prior's Ford, for three years. And then she came to Rushbrooke Hill, where the PCC accepted her, but you refused to recognise her.'

'Yes, to my shame that's true. But how on earth did you find out all that?'

'Well, you see, Colonel Calderdale,' said Noel Greenspan, 'we are private investigators, and we have our contacts in many spheres of life. Mrs McArthur is also blessed with a photographic memory. What we'd now like to hear from you is your connection with the Reverend Julian Stringer, whom Renfield mentioned in that note. We know something about him. So let's hear the full story, mind. No shilly-shallying.'

When Nigel had finished his sorry tale, the pair sat in silence for a while, just looking at him. They were both of them a bit unnerving, but Frank Renfield had been right. These two were the goods.

'Very well, Colonel,' said Noel Greenspan. 'We'll be delighted to undertake this research for you. We have close access to the two detectives investigating the Reverend Stacey's death — Detective Inspector French and Sergeant Edwards — and we'd expect you to grant us permission to share any findings with them.'

'Absolutely. So I can leave the matter in your hands?'

'You can. Our fee will be £1500, plus expenses.'

When the colonel had gone, Chloe said, 'He was very impressed by our research into his murdered vicar.'

'Yes, indeed,' said Noel, 'and yet all you did was consult *Crockford's Clerical Directory* in the reference library. He could have done that himself.'

Noel Greenspan levered himself from behind his desk, and made for the door.

'I'm going down now to Jubilee House to speak to Glyn Edwards. I know that he's been on the track of the Reverend Julian Stringer, and I'd like to hear what he's found out, as well as alerting him to the fact that we two are also on the case.'

'You know, Noel,' said Chloe, 'that murder was a particularly vile act — pure evil, in my book. And I object to a fellow woman being murdered just because she dares to seek parity with men. So let's get down to business.'

'Do you strive to seek parity with me?' enquired Noel.

'You're a different matter entirely,' said Noel's partner.

7. A TRAIL OF TRAGEDIES

'Stacey was a very clever girl, Mr Greenspan. She left here with excellent A-level results and a foundation scholarship to Latimer College, Cambridge,' said Rebecca Thorne. The headmistress's study at Elm Grove High School for Girls was furnished like an elegant sitting room, with no signs of exercise books, intrusive computers, or anything as passé as chalk. That, Noel Greenspan guessed, was how the parents liked it.

He had had no trouble in locating the private secondary school where Stacey Williams had been educated. Elm Grove was a leafy London suburb, housed in a mix of old and modern buildings, all standing in extensive grounds with tennis courts and well-tended playing fields.

'Was she a popular pupil?'

'Yes, I think she was well liked by both girls and staff. Of course, it's many years ago that she was here. 1985 to 1991. But I remember her well.'

Miss Thorne was a slim, haggardly handsome woman with well-tended grey hair, and a flair for dressing in a way that would please the fee-paying parents of her pupils. She had received Noel Greenspan with courtesy, but he detected a certain wry watchfulness in her manner. She would require careful handling.

'I'm sure that you have heard that she was most cruelly murdered not many weeks since,' said Noel. 'Poisoned at the altar while celebrating Holy Communion.'

Miss Thorne gave a shudder of distaste, as if vexed that one of her girls should have been so inconsiderate as to get herself murdered. Things of that nature reflected no glory on Elm Grove High School.

'As far as you can recollect, Miss Thorne, did Stacey Williams show any strong interest in religion while she was here?'

'She was a religious girl — belief came naturally to her, I think. And while she was popular, as I say, she began to evince a dogmatism over matters of religion that was not pleasing. To be fully educated, Mr Greenspan, you need to have the ability to see all sides of a question — oh, not to end up believing nothing, but to be aware at least that others' beliefs, while contradicting yours, are sincerely held. Dogmatism in the young can be a cause of real concern.'

At last! Here was something that gave a clue to Stacey Williams's later troubles. This shrewd teacher of youth had detected a flaw in the otherwise laudable pupil who had won a scholarship to Cambridge.

'Any trouble with boys?'

That had been an attempt at a frontal assault, but it failed. Miss Thorne laughed, and her stern features relaxed.

'Boys? No, not Stacey. I don't think she was interested in boys at all. Her parents were very High Church, and she followed in their footsteps. Perhaps she didn't have the imagination for rebellion, but I think even then she had discerned a vocation to the single life, either as a nun, or as a clergywoman in the Anglican Church. But that dogmatism — that rigidity of belief, well, things like that can lead a person along very dangerous paths.'

'It was very good of you to see me, Miss Thorne,' said Noel Greenspan. 'I would like to assure you that although I am a private detective, I am working in full cooperation with the police. We have not yet found out who murdered the

Reverend Stacey Williams, but what you've told me today has been invaluable.'

It was time to bid the headmistress farewell, and find a local pub where he could get a pint and a pie.

'Stay to lunch,' said Miss Thorne unexpectedly. 'We've good food here, and you've come a long way to visit us. And I've just remembered something — something involving Stacey when she was at Latimer College. It was trouble with another girl. I'm not sure of the detail, but you might like to extend your enquiry to Cambridge.'

* * *

'Didn't your friend Maud Armitage have some kind of job at Latimer College?' asked Noel Greenspan. 'You're still in touch with her, aren't you? Would you like to pay her a visit, all expenses paid? She may be able to tell you what happened to Stacey Williams and another undergraduate there.'

'I'd love to see Maud again,' said Chloe. 'It's years since I saw her. She was a part-time bedmaker at Latimer while she was studying at one of the Cambridge secretarial colleges, so if there was a scandal involving Stacey Williams, she'd know about it.'

'Bedmaker?'

'Yes, it's the name given to the women who look after the students' rooms. Similar to the scouts in Oxford colleges. When she qualified, Maud got an admin post with Cambridge University Press, and made Cambridge her permanent home. Yes, I'd love to see her again. Maybe I'll drive up.'

'Cambridge is "ten leagues beyond man's life", as Shakespeare said. Why not go by train? After all, Colonel Nigel Calderdale will be footing the bill.'

* * *

Maud Armitage lived in a comfortable retirement complex a few miles from Trumpington. A well-preserved woman in her seventies, she had shown delight at meeting her old friend once again.

'I often think of that awful boarding school that we both survived,' she said. 'We were there in different decades, but the suffering never varied. I thought it would have been closed down years ago, but apparently it's still thriving — under different management, I hasten to add. And then we both worked together for that lovely old firm of solicitors here in Cambridge until you were lured away to follow in the footsteps of Sherlock Holmes!

'But I'm intrigued to know why you've come to visit me, apart from renewing the pleasure of my company. You said very little in your letter.'

'I want you to cast your mind back to the 1990s, when you were still a part-time bedmaker at Latimer College. And I want you to think in particular of one of the undergraduates there, a girl called Stacey Williams.'

'Oh, dear, poor Stacey! Murdered at the altar. Horrible. When I read about it in the paper, I could hardly believe that it was the Stacey Williams I'd known at Latimer. But of course, it was. Some of the papers hinted at black magic and Satanic rites.'

'Can you recall her as an undergraduate?' asked Chloe.

'Indeed I can. She was a very intelligent, lively girl, and a hard worker without appearing to be a swot. She was very religious, and while she was regular in attending the college chapel, she preferred to haunt the various Anglo-Catholic churches in the town and beyond. She'd go out with a group of like-minded friends on what used to be called "church crawls".'

'I've heard that there was trouble over some girl—'

'It was nonsense!' Maud Armitage flushed with indignation. 'Who told you about that? Girls form romantic friendships. There's nothing odd or peculiar about that. And this girl — she was a pretty, rather shy young lady with long dark hair and gentle eyes. She fell for Stacey in a big way, and wanted them to study together, even though they were reading different subjects. She bought Stacey flowers and chocolates, which Stacey would give away to us bedmakers.'

'I wonder if that was her way of showing her rejection of that girl's affection?' said Chloe. 'Latimer was the last of the Cambridge women's colleges, wasn't it?'

'They take men there now. But not in those days. Anyway, things came to a head one November night in Michaelmas term. Apparently, this girl had brought yet another unwanted present for Stacey, and Stacey had finally had enough. A more sensitive girl might have reacted differently, but Stacey was very obviously distraught at the other girl's clinging devotion. She told her that she never wanted to see her again, and that she should pray to the Lord for forgiveness. Forgiveness for *what*, I don't know. Girls of that age haven't anything really serious to confess, God knows.'

For a moment Chloe's friend seemed caught up in her memories. Then she shook her head sadly.

'I think that other girl would have grown out of that particular crush with a bit of gentle handling and moved on to someone who could return her feelings,' she said, 'but Stacey wasn't the gentle type. So there it is. I don't think anything actually *happened*, mind. Nothing "unnatural", as we used to say at the time. Phil — there, I've mentioned her name, though I tried not to — Phil was quite forthright, though shy, as I said, and Stacey was a straightforward and devout young woman who was repelled and rather frightened by Phil's advances.'

'What happened to Phil?'

'She drowned in the River Cam. It was brought in as death by misadventure, but some people thought differently. Stacey Williams was not to blame, and had the common sense not to blame herself. She went on to get a very good degree, and fulfilled her ambition to become a vicar.'

On the train journey back to London, Chloe McArthur sat back in her seat and thought about what Maud Armitage had told her. A picture of Stacey Williams was beginning to form in her mind. She was extremely religious, and part of a sect of Christianity that deemed same-sex attraction 'unnatural', deeply sinful. She seemed not to have had any boyfriends, and had never married. Maud Armitage had been adamant that a romantic attachment had been obvious only on Phil's side, but what if that attraction had been there in Stacey, too?

Might not Stacey's violent rebuttal of the other girl's affection indicate that she had in fact fallen for her devotee, and was determined to resist at all costs? Stacey Williams saw things in black and white. She had been sustained by a strong faith, but there had been little evidence of charity. What had happened to her in the parishes where she had served? It was going to be necessary to delve deeper. More than one person might have been after Stacey's blood.

* * *

'So,' said Noel Greenspan, 'Stacey Williams had a tragedy in her past. I wonder if she mended her ways, or if she continued to be an abrasive character?'

'A dangerous quality in a vicar,' Chloe remarked.

'Your visit to Cambridge certainly paid dividends, as did my interview with Rebecca Thorne, Stacey's old headmistress. But I think we need to find out a bit more before we compile a report for Colonel Nigel Calderdale. I wonder whether it's time to bring Lance Middleton into the investigation? Stacey was resident in London, both as a student and a clergywoman, for well over ten years before she moved to a country parish, Prior's Ford — I wonder why she did that? She was only there for three years before she moved again to Rushbrooke Hill.'

'Yes, that point struck me,' said Chloe McArthur. 'Why did she move there? And did anything peculiar happen during those three years?'

'We might visit Prior's Ford and do some digging there. And in the meantime, since Lance is based in London,' said Noel, 'and knows his way around all its highways and byways, we could ask for his assistance there.'

'I'll phone him now. He should be at home in his chambers in Lincoln's Inn at this time of day. I'll whet his curiosity and his appetite, while offering as a starter a modest fee from Colonel Calderdale's bounty.'

'Where do you propose to send him?'

'I think it's time we had a chat with Stacey's parents. I've been in contact with Glyn Edwards, who told me that the parents appeared at the inquest, which was held in Rushbrooke Hill village hall. They gave evidence of identification, answered a few questions, and then left immediately for London. Apparently they had never visited Stacey in her final parish, and certainly showed not the slightest interest in the church when they were there. And then, Glyn told me, as soon as they'd released Stacey's body, they turned up with a closed undertaker's van and whisked her off to London. Again, no interest in the church, the village, or any of Stacey's colleagues there.'

'What do we know about them?'

'While you were away in Cambridge, I looked them up. Stanley and Elizabeth Williams, both in their sixties. He's a chartered accountant, still working from home. It seems he has a very good reputation. She's a recently retired music teacher. Nice people, by the sound of it. They live in Maida Vale.'

'What do you think they'll make of Lance Middleton? He can be quite overwhelming to people who don't know him well. That voice, and his propensity for chatter. And he's bordering on the obese—'

'He's fat,' said Noel. 'He eats too much, but his brain's as sharp as a pin — well, you know that. He's been involved in some very hectic adventures with us. I think they'll be slightly in awe of him, but after all Mr Williams is a professional man himself, the type of man, I suppose, who offers you a nice glass of sherry when you call on him.'

'You're not supposed to say somebody's fat,' said Chloe. 'You're supposed to say that he has body-mass issues.'

'I stand corrected,' said Noel Greenspan. 'Do you think I have body-mass issues?'

'Decidedly. But I know that you'll do nothing about it, and neither will Lance. That's life.'

* * *

The Williamses lived in a very attractive detached house in Maida Vale. There was a well-tended front lawn with neat flowerbeds and an extensive greenhouse in the long back garden. Stanley Williams was a smartly dressed, clean-shaven man with grey hair turning white. He wore glasses, the right lens of which had been frosted, suggesting that he had lost an eye. Elizabeth Williams was a quiet woman wearing a floral dress and a necklace of cultured pearls.

There was a grand piano in the spacious sitting room, and Lance saw a number of photographs in silver frames standing on it. There was a baby in a nappy lying on a rug, a smiling young woman in academic dress, and the same young woman in the robes of an Anglican priest. Finally, there was another photograph of her standing in a garden with an attractive young man. Lance wondered who he was. They were, he realised, pictures of Stacey Williams, although he had never seen her in person.

'This is an excellent sherry, Mr Williams,' said Lance Middleton. 'I do feel it's a very civilised habit to enjoy a glass or two mid-morning.'

'I'm glad you like it,' said Stanley Williams. 'And you're a QC? Do you work with the police? My wife and I are intrigued why you should want to visit us.'

'I work with a firm of private investigators — they have a close relationship with the police,' said Lance. 'I've been asked to look into Stacey's background in London, to see if I can shed any light on this terrible crime.'

'She was our only child,' said Mr Williams. 'We're — we're *numbed*, both of us, over what happened to her. Such a clever girl, and never rebellious while she was at home with us. My wife and I are devout Anglo-Catholics — I'm master of ceremonies at St Polycarp's — and Stacey took after us in being devoted to the Catholic side of the Church of England.'

'I believe that many Anglo-Catholics don't believe that women can be priests,' said Lance.

'It's true, I didn't myself, but when I saw Stacey's growing vocation to the sacred ministry, I revised my ideas. It was not easy for her, Mr Middleton, but she persevered, and never lost her faith. While she was at Cambridge she even wondered whether she had a vocation to the religious life — becoming a nun. She even had an interview with the Prioress of Highfield Convent. If anyone was called by God to the ministry, our Stacey was.'

'It was disgraceful!' Mrs Williams's voice quivered with indignation. 'At both her ordinations — to the diaconate and the priesthood — there were boos and cries of "shame!" from people planted in the congregation. That's why we wouldn't visit any church where she served, would we, Stanley? And when she was murdered at that church in Oldshire, we just turned up for the inquest, and to collect her body. She's buried in Kensal Green Cemetery.'

'I'm very sorry,' said Lance, 'more sorry than I can say. It's not theology, it's misogyny, pure and simple. From what I understand she took it rather well when it happened, which was rare until she arrived at her final parish. What I want to ask you is this: my colleagues uncovered a police report of a disturbance at your house — this would have been after Stacey had graduated, I think. Could you tell me anything about it?'

The parents looked at each other, and Lance saw some kind of understanding pass between them.

'Stacey was living with us at the time. Emma Fletcher turned up here shouting abuse after — well, she made a show of herself and us by screaming that she'd get her revenge on Stacey. We called the police, and they came and moved her on. That was over twenty years ago. And nothing came of it, and poor Emma drowned in the park lake a year later.'

'Perhaps you've also seen police reports about the abusive letters,' said Stacey's father, 'letters from fanatics. Some were signed, others were anonymous. There was a group of particularly vicious people called the Warriors of Christ, led by a man called Stringer, who I believe is a defrocked clergyman. The letters stopped after I threatened legal action. But he's still active, and had begun to persecute Stacey at Rushbrooke Hill.'

'Yes, the police know all about the Reverend Julian Stringer. But tell me, who was this Emma Fletcher, who shouted abuse outside your house, and drowned in the park lake?'

Stanley Williams stirred in his chair uneasily.

'Oh, why drag that business up? It was years ago, and we've forgiven poor Emma.'

'I think we should tell him, Stanley,' said Elizabeth Williams. 'What harm can it do now?'

Mr Williams sighed. Lance saw him glance at the piano, and sensed that he was looking at the photograph of his daughter standing in a garden with an attractive young man.

'When Stacey was studying for her diploma in Theology at London University, she met a young man called Mark Fletcher. That's him, in that picture there. He was a lovely chap, or so we thought, and he and Stacey were married in 1995.

'Well, he turned out to be an alcoholic, and when he was drunk he was a demon. He used to knock Stacey about, even after she had taken Holy Orders. He was always remorseful when he'd sobered up, but it became clear to us both that Stacey's life and career would be ruined if she stayed with him. Their marriage dragged on for three years, and then quite suddenly Mark died.'

'Died?'

'Yes, he took bad at a meal, and died of food poisoning. He was only twenty-four. So we didn't talk about her marriage, and neither did Stacey. She was a widow, but everybody assumed that she was single. And so she was, for the rest of her life.'

'And Emma Fletcher was Mark's mother?'

'His sister. It was a very trying time, to say the least. Well, they're all gone now.'

There it was again: a trail of wreckage in her wake. This time a young husband, and then his sister, drowned in a park lake. Suicide? Perhaps.

It was an easy matter for Lance to find the records of the two deaths. In Mark Fletcher's case, it was accidental death, consequent on food poisoning. His wife had left him a salad, consisting of tinned salmon, lettuce and tomato, as she would be out at a meeting when he returned from work. A post-mortem revealed that he had died of botulism, derived from infected salmon.

His sister, Emma Fletcher, was given a verdict of 'found drowned', no positive reasons being found to explain how she had fallen into the water of the park lake. Once again, Lance Middleton asked himself the question: suicide? To which he added the same proviso: perhaps.

* * *

Highfield Convent of the Sisters of Mary was situated near the pleasant town of Esher. It had been built in the Gothic style with money provided by a wealthy Victorian lady whose two daughters had taken the veil there. It was an Anglican foundation which still managed to attract vocations even in these secular times.

Mother Agnes Mary, the prioress, received Lance Middleton in the convent parlour, where she was busy embroidering a stole. She was a very old lady, dressed in the traditional robes of a nun. *No secular dress for her!* thought Lance. *Sister Agnes Mary is a nun of the old school.*

'Yes, Mr Middleton, Stacey Williams would often come on retreat here for a few days when the pressures of parish work proved too much.' The prioress's voice came small and quavering. She wore strong spectacles, and was obviously near-sighted, perhaps as a result of the fine stitching needed to produce the embroidered vestments for which she and her sisters, apparently, were celebrated.

'And now she is murdered,' said the prioress. 'She is a martyr for the faith, and God will have received her straight away into heaven. But you've not come here, have you, to hear me preach, or to give you a lesson in theology. What can I do for you?'

'I have been talking to Stacey's parents, Reverend Mother, and they told me that when she was at Cambridge she came here to see whether or not she had a vocation to the religious life.'

The prioress gave him a shrewd glance and pushed the embroidery aside.

'Some people carry the makings of their own ruin within them,' she said. 'I think Stacey may have been one such person. She came here to test her vocation in the early nineties — 1992, I think. I was prioress even then. I'm a great age now, but you know the old saying: "a creaking gate lasts longest".

'Well, she soon settled down to convent life, learning all about obedience to me, to the novice mistress, and other senior sisters. She was enthusiastic about undertaking the manual work that we insist on here, and when she joined in the services in chapel, her devotion to the traditional liturgy we used here — it was all in Latin, then — was particularly apparent.'

Mother Agnes Mary stopped speaking, and for a while seemed absorbed in her memories.

'But she never became a nun,' said Lance.

'No, she never became a nun. She was an ideal candidate for the veil as long as she could have her own way, but if anyone crossed her, well, that was a different matter. I don't mean that she was openly disobedient. But if the novice mistress rebuked her, I would see her flush with anger, while doing what she had been told to do. I saw how she began to exert her influence over our little choir, gradually making the leader defer to her suggestions. Things like that, which told me that her imagined vocation did not come from God, or truly from her heart. She was, I think, in love with an *idea*, but would have found the mundane aspects of our life here intolerable after a while.

'I called her to a final interview, and asked her how she regarded the idea of life in an enclosed convent. She began

to talk to me as though convent life involved a ladder of pro-
motions. "If I were to become novice mistress, this is what
I'd do . . . I would work hard until I was qualified to become
sub-prioress, and then I would do such and such." She was
absorbed entirely with herself, and had no concept of emp-
tying herself, and taking on the form of a servant. So I told
her that we didn't discern a true vocation in her case, and I
think she gave an inward sigh of relief.

'But she had genuinely liked her time here, and has come
here on conducted retreats many times. And we all welcomed
her. But the cloistered life, Mr Middleton, was not for her.'

* * *

One sunny summer morning the church at Rushbrooke
Hill was reconsecrated. There was a grand turnout of the
villagers to see the two bishops — Bishop Poindexter and
his suffragan, Michael Sandford, Bishop of Bedworth. Nigel
Calderdale took a prominent place in his family pew, which
he shared with Bishop Sandford's wife and young children.

Because the diocesan bishop was present, the service was
not as Papalist as usual, but there was plenty of incense burnt
and holy water splashed about. Bishop Poindexter, clad in
cope and mitre, read a number of very long prayers. Michael
Sandford then celebrated the first Mass at the reconsecrated
altar, assisted by a team of earnest servers imported from the
theological college at Oldminster. Alan Shirtcliffe had agreed
to that concession because the bishop had wanted it, but the
team of girl servers that Stacey Williams had gathered had
all returned with their parents' blessing, and Alan made it
clear that their position at Holy Trinity was non-negotiable.

When it was all over, Dr John Miller accepted Nigel
Calderdale's invitation to lunch at Rushbrooke House.

'I know that they've laid on a lavish buffet in the church
hall,' said Nigel. 'But somehow I felt the need to make myself
scarce until the dignitaries have packed up and gone.'

'What did you think of the service?' asked John Miller.

'I thought it was very impressive. You know that the bishop's always thought we were a bit excessive here? Maybe we'll tone things down a bit in future, and make the place more recognisably Anglican.'

'That's quite a revolutionary thought, coming from you!'

'Yes, maybe. But I really did feel that the Devil had been driven out of the place this morning. The return to holiness was palpable. And I'm glad to say that there were no so-called "demonstrators" present to sully the proceeds. There were also two uniformed police officers stationed at the door, which may have helped, I suppose.'

'So we now have our church back,' said John Miller. 'We've planned a joint thanksgiving service with the Methodists, who gave us the hospitality of their church hall for the last month. It was the least we could do.'

'Thank God I came to my senses before it was too late,' said Nigel. 'I feel more myself at last, now that that appalling clergyman has disappeared. What on earth possessed me to throw in my lot with him and his raggle-taggle followers?'

'Maybe it was the Devil,' said John. 'But it's all over, now, Nigel, and it's time for us to start scouting around for a new vicar. Give it another month, and things should be back to normal.

'But to change the subject for a moment. This is a very nice lunch, but it's not been cooked by Ruth Page, has it? Where *is* Ruth, by the way?'

John had the satisfaction of seeing his friend blush to the roots of his hair. As a keen observer of parish life, he had noticed that Nigel and Rose Talmadge were well on the road to becoming an item.

'Damn you, John, I can't keep any secret from you. Rose and I are contemplating marriage. Why shouldn't we? I'm a widower, she's a respectable spinster. So, yes, why shouldn't we? As for Ruth, she's seen the way things are shaping, and has handed in her resignation, and is going as live-in nanny-cum-housekeeper with Mr and Mrs Meredith Smith at Castle Gate.'

'My congratulations to you both,' said John. 'Now let me just tell you a few things that you've missed while you were — er — indisposed. Alan Shirtcliffe has continued to hold the PCC together with a firm hand, ably assisted by Tony Savidge. Tony told me that they are both determined to make sure that the council is never again hijacked by unsettling interest groups.'

'Including me, I suppose.'

'Well, yes, if you regard yourself as a group. Incidentally, Amanda Waters has decided to offer herself as an ordinand under the tutelage of the Bishop of Bedworth. I think it's very brave of her, all things considered, but she's had a lot of encouragement from Megan Shirtcliffe.'

'Oh,' Nigel spluttered. 'Amanda? I didn't know she . . .' He seemed lost for words.

'As you know,' John went on quickly, 'we've long been in need of a competent treasurer, and I'm delighted to say that Sally Eardley has agreed to accept the office. It turns out that she is a businesswoman in her own right, and more than capable of looking after the parish finances. So here's to a new era for Holy Trinity!'

'Yes, indeed,' said Nigel Calderdale. 'But I'll never forget that poor woman, and the vile things that were done to her. May she rest in peace, and rise in glory!'

8. JOHN THE BAPTIST, PADDINGTON

Lance Middleton sat in his car and looked up at the towering red-brick church of St John the Baptist, Paddington. It stood in an area of depressed high-rise flats, and streets of terrace houses, with a few corner shops, some with their windows boarded up. He noted that some small panes in one of the long stained-glass windows were missing, victims to what some poet or other had described as 'the bitter, snarling derisive stone'. It was here that the Reverend Stacey Williams had ministered as vicar for ten years.

This parish was one of the High Church 'shrines' familiar to most Anglo-Catholics in the London diocese. Built in 1880, it was the work of the Victorian architect John Loughborough Pearson.

Leaving his car, Lance made his way to the nearby vicarage, an elegant house also designed by Pearson, and rang the bell. The door was answered by a pleasant, grey-haired lady in a flowered smock.

'Mr Middleton? Father's expecting you. I'm Agnes Jones, his housekeeper.'

The entrance hall was dominated by a life-size statue of the Virgin Mary. The house exuded a faint aroma of beeswax and incense. Throwing open a door to the left, Agnes Jones announced him, and quietly left the room. A balding, heavy man in a lived-in cassock rose from a chair to greet him. He limped heavily, and it came as a slight shock to Lance to realise that the vicar had a false leg.

'Pleased and intrigued to meet you, Mr Middleton. I got your note saying that you wanted to see me, and talk about the Reverend Miss Stacey Williams. Terrible. A terrible business. I had a Requiem Mass for her here — the proper thing, you know, with a catafalque, and black vestments. A lot of the Affirming Catholicism people came. The Bishop of Willesden presided in the sanctuary.'

Father Hallowes had a powerful but pleasant voice, and a natural gift for making any visitor feel at home. He limped across the room, and opened a cabinet, from which he extracted a bottle of sherry and two glasses.

'Not too early, I hope? This is a thirty-year-old *Bodegas Tradicion.*'

'Vicar,' cried Lance Middleton, 'you're a man after my own heart!'

They sat in battered but comfortable leather armchairs on either side of an elaborate cast-iron fireplace, and Father Hallowes looked a question.

'I'd like to know more about the Reverend Stacey Williams's ten-year incumbency,' said Lance. 'We have not yet found out who murdered her, and why. I'm just wondering whether I could find any clues from her time here. I gather she was very successful.'

'She was,' said Father Hallowes. 'She became the vicar in 2004, when the parish was just about on its last legs. I was a curate at All Saints, Margaret Street, in those days, but I got to know Stacey well. It was a bold thing for a woman in Holy Orders to do at that time, as there was a very strong bias against female clergy. I must admit that I shared that bias myself. But it was impossible not to fall under Stacey's spell. I came here one Sunday to see what she got up to, and I found her celebrating a Solemn Mass quite impeccably, using the Roman Missal, proper vestments, the lot. Her sermon was a riveting call to renewal, delivered in confident and ringing tones. I was quickly converted!

'During her ministry she built up a quite remarkable congregation of devoted parishioners. She established a flourishing youth group, a men's fellowship, one of the earliest food banks in London — oh, all sorts of things. There was daily Mass, and the Angelus at noon — she'd ring the bell herself — and after a year she introduced sung vespers, which attracted quite a following, including me.'

He laughed.

'A lot of it was technically interdict, but nobody felt like interfering with her. Persecuting Anglo-Catholics had rather gone out of fashion.'

'But there was still prejudice against a female vicar,' said Lance.

'Oh, yes, plenty of that. There was the occasional demonstration — people with banners shouting insults — but Stacey braved them all. She was a valiant, strong-willed woman, who refused to let herself be defeated by these fanatics.'

'Was she ever bothered by an outfit called the Warriors of Christ? They were run by a clergyman called Julian Stringer.'

'I've not heard of that group, though his name strikes a rather cracked bell. We had enough fanatics of our own here in London to go around.'

'And what about you, Father? Did you experience any prejudice?'

'Me? I lost a few fair-weather friends because of my defence of Stacey. I didn't care. Things were changing, and there are times when one must come to terms with change. Have another glass of sherry.'

'Thank you. Let me get it for us — save you getting up. Did she minister here all alone?'

'Oh, no. After a year, the bishop sent her a curate, a young man who fitted in very nicely. He left after three years to accept a living somewhere up north. And then, in 2014, she left, to take up a country living somewhere in Hampshire.

I think she was growing tired of what you might call inner-city ministry. And that's when *I* came. I won't pretend that I was in the same league as Stacey. I've done what I can, but I'm hampered by this leg — I lost it in a road accident, and it's been a real trouble to me ever since.'

Father Hallowes sat in silence for a while, evidently preoccupied with his own thoughts. Then he came back to the present, and laughed ruefully.

'I don't think we'll be open for much longer,' he said. 'I think the bishop will close us down. Stacey brought life to the parish. Since she left, it's become a sort of mausoleum. I've been offered the chaplaincy of a convent in Sussex, so when the bishop acts, I'll have somewhere to go.'

He rose with some difficulty from his chair, and Lance sensed that the interview was over.

'And she left because she had tired of urban ministry?'

Father Hallowes sighed. He looked vexed, but more with himself than with Lance.

'Before you go,' he said, 'go through to the kitchen and have a talk with Agnes. She's lived in this part of Paddington for years, and has her ear close to the ground. She may tell you things that it would be unprofessional of me to mention.'

* * *

'We were horrified when we read about it in the paper, Mr Middleton. Who could have done such a wicked thing?'

It was reassuringly comfortable in the vicarage kitchen, where Agnes Jones insisted on Lance sampling her home-baked Danish pastries, to be washed down with properly percolated coffee. Mrs Jones settled herself down in her chair at the kitchen table. Lance realised that his best way of opening the conversation was to say nothing, and leave his hostess to start the proceedings. There must have been a specific reason for the vicar having pointed Lance in her direction.

'Yes, it was a terrible thing to hear about. She was such a good woman, very highly principled. She believed in going

87

by the book. Some things were right, and other things were wrong, and there was no halfway house in between.'

In a moment, thought Lance, she'll tell me the true reason why Stacey left the parish after ten years.

'It was very sad,' Agnes Jones continued. 'She had done so well here, and was respected by everyone. Well, there was a poor couple lived in this parish, not three streets away from here. Their name was Dwyer. James and Margaret Dwyer. He was a roofer by trade, but bad health had put him out of work, and they were living on benefits. They came to church when they were able, which wasn't often, I must admit, but they were good people, both of them.

'Margaret Dwyer had the added burden of a sister confined to a psychiatric hospital — what we used to call an asylum. So she looked after her ailing husband, and visited her sister whenever she was able.'

'Were they an elderly couple?' asked Lance.

'Oh, no, they were only in their thirties, but they were battered and bruised by poverty, so I may have made them sound older than they were. *He* was certainly old before his time. They had a little girl called Ellie, a toddler. Now, what's the best way of explaining all this to you? Let me see . . .

'James Dwyer had a friend, a fellow roofer, who belonged to a little tin tabernacle church not far from here. An independent church, it was, with a pastor, as they called him, who was a bit of a ranter, but not a bad chap. And this friend of James Dwyer asked him whether Ellie had been baptised yet, and when James said no, this man told him that if Ellie died unbaptised, she would go to hell.'

'I don't know any church that teaches that,' said Lance hotly.

'Neither do I, Mr Middleton, and I don't suppose the tabernacle really taught that, but it's what this friend of James Dwyer evidently believed. The upshot of it was, that James and Margaret came to see Stacey, who . . .'

Agnes Jones looked vexed. Lance soon found out why.

'She should have told those two that what that man said was nonsense, but she was such a stickler for form and order, that instead of reassuring them, she began to plan their daughter's baptism on the spot. They were to come to church every Sunday for three weeks, and find two people willing to stand as godparents, etc, etc. I'm sure that most of what she told them went over their heads, but they did what Stacey told them.'

Lance was wondering where all this was leading to.

'And so little Ellie was baptised?'

'No, she wasn't. Because just a week before the baptism, Ellie fell into convulsions, and died. This was in 2010. You don't expect things like that to happen in modern times. I told you that neither of them knew much about the Church and its teachings, and it was James Dwyer's sad fate to believe what his friend told him. He was convinced, you see, that Stacey's delay in baptising their baby had sent her little soul to hell.'

'Poor man,' said Lance. 'And that's the reason why Stacey left the parish?'

'No, there's more, Mr Middleton. James Dwyer survived his daughter's death by three days. And then he hanged himself.'

'Good God!' cried Lance. 'Poor, wretched man. No wonder Stacey felt obliged to leave the parish after that.'

'There's more,' said Agnes Jones, 'when Stacey heard that James Dwyer had committed suicide, she at first refused to bury him in consecrated ground, or allow him to be buried with his unbaptised but innocent daughter. And that *did* cause a scandal! The whole neighbourhood was up in arms, and the archdeacon came to compel Stacey to bury her dead parishioner.'

'And did she?'

'Yes, but she made sure that he was buried on the north side of the church, where suicides were buried in the old days, and with curtailed rites. It was all done according to the book, but it was the end of the line for Stacey. People still came to church, and treated her civilly, but all the love had gone, to be replaced by cold respect. Compassion, Mr Middleton, that's what you need if you're going to put yourself in care of souls. Anyway, the Bishop of London sent Stacey on sabbatical, a kind of paid holiday, and provided a substitute, a young curate called Arthur Downs. And the first thing he did was to bury little Ellie with her father, sprinkling holy water on the two coffins. It was — it was like an exorcism, Mr Middleton. Stacey was supposed to come back, but never returned. I think the Bishop of London must have prevailed on her to move on. Mr Downs stayed to hold the fort, and then Father Hallowes came.'

For the first time since she began her story, Agnes Jones broke out into a smile.

'He's a big-hearted man, with a pastoral heart, as we say, and a great liking for his food and drink! He's in constant pain with that leg, but never complains. We'll miss him when it's time for him to go.'

'Were you Stacey's housekeeper?' asked Lance.

'No, she managed by herself, with some help from a local girl. But she got herself a housekeeper in her last couple of years here. A quiet, washed-out sort of woman, she was. I came here to look after Father Hallowes after my husband died. We don't usually talk about all this, Mr Middleton, because it's ancient history now, and Stacey did a great deal to restore this church and parish. Still, what happened to her was a tragedy, and she left a couple of tragedies behind her when she left.'

'What happened to Ellie's mother?'

'Margaret Dwyer? She moved away to the town where her sister was in the asylum — I don't know where it was — and just a year after that, she died of cancer. She was only thirty-three.'

* * *

On his way back to Lincoln's Inn, Lance Middleton thought about Ellie and her parents, all now dead, and he thought of Typhoid Mary, the domestic cook in the Edwardian era who was a carrier of typhoid leading to deaths in places where she worked, without ever suffering from it herself. Stacey Williams had been like that: wherever she had been, she had left a trail of deaths behind her, without perhaps being consciously responsible for any of them. But Lance was more and more convinced that it was someone from her past who had plotted her death in revenge for one of those earlier deaths. All this nonsense of demons and wicked spirits was nothing more than a smokescreen.

Time to report to Noel and Chloe.

* * *

Chloe McArthur sat at a computer terminal in the National Archives at Kew, sifting through records of births and deaths. Her visit with Noel to Stacey's previous parish had proved unedifying. Prior's Ford was a chocolate-box hamlet — a church and vicarage, a couple of thatched cottages and not much more than that. The surrounding fields were largely filled with solar panels rather than animals or crops. When they'd stopped the car outside the church and switched off the engine, the place was deadly quiet. It was easy to see why Stacey had moved on.

They had found the vicarage vacant, with a note on the door directing callers to the diocese office in Portsmouth, and there was nobody at the church, which was locked. One of the cottages, the Beeches, was also empty, but the door of the other opened at their knock, and a grey-haired dame peered at them kindly over half-moon spectacles, but had turned out not to speak a word of English. They had given it up as a bad job, and Chloe had left a message for the diocese office to return her call without much hope of an answer.

She had found the birth certificate of Ellie Dwyer, and then the certificate of her death at the age of twenty-one months. A deeper search in facsimiles of London parish records had come up with a photocopy of a document recording Ellie's burial with her father at the church of St John the Baptist, Paddington. It proved to be something more than a mere soulless record, for someone had written in pencil in one of the margins: *I ordered the father's coffin to be exposed, so that I could sprinkle it with holy water. Then the baby's little coffin was placed on top of it. — AD.*

AD . . . That would be the initials of Arthur Downs, the young curate who had held the fort at St John the Baptist while Stacey was on her sabbatical. That he had thought fit to make that statement on an official document showed how outraged this clergyman had been at Stacey's callous addiction to the rule book.

Chloe's next task was to search for any documents relating to Ellie's mother, Margaret Dwyer. Over a period of several hours she called up document after document, eventually finding Margaret's birth certificate dated 14 April 1978. Daughter of Peter Grint, publican, and Ethel Grint, housewife. Grint? Where had she heard that name before? It would come back to her.

Margaret Dwyer's death certificate showed that she had died in the Royal Bolton Hospital, Lancashire, the cause of death being cancer. At her own wish she had been cremated, and her ashes scattered at the crematorium. Evidently she had not wanted to be buried with her husband and baby.

Lance Middleton had been told that after her daughter's death Margaret Dwyer had gone to live near her sister, who was a patient in a mental hospital. Chloe now knew that the hospital in question must be in or near Bolton. It was time for her to make a train journey to Lancashire.

* * *

'I'm sure you'll understand, Mrs McArthur, that a patient's records remain confidential even after they've been discharged.'

Chloe had been prepared for this statement when she had arrived at Hill View Psychiatric Unit, a complex of modern buildings a mile or two from Bolton. Sister Hackett, a woman in her early forties, was very obviously dedicated to her vocation. Her glass-walled office looked out on to an eerily silent corridor along which a white-coated doctor would walk from time to time.

Chloe saw that Sister Hackett was wearing a wedding ring. On her desk was a framed photograph of herself with a cheerful-looking man and two young children, a boy and a girl. This woman could be handled through a personal approach, though it would be necessary to tell a few fibs in order to make her reveal what she knew. Fibs? No, *lies*. Why not face up to the truth?

'Absolutely, Sister,' said Chloe, 'I fully understand. There are ethical codes to be followed. We have such codes in our profession as detectives, especially when we have been retained by — well, I cannot name names. No, the reason I'm here today is to trace the only living relative of the late James Dwyer, who died by his own hand in 2010.'

'Yes, she told me all about that,' said Sister Hackett. 'Wasn't it dreadful? And the baby girl, too. The sister would come here to visit our patient, and we'd sometimes have a five-minute chat about family matters. Poor woman! She died of cancer, leaving our patient entirely alone with her thoughts and her memories.'

'It turns out,' said Chloe, blushing in spite of herself, 'that James Dwyer had a great-uncle in Australia, who died recently, and they found an old will in which he'd left his fortune to James. This has only recently come to light, you understand. And our research has shown us that your patient is the only living relative of the great-uncle. That's why we're so anxious to trace her.'

'How — how much did this great-uncle leave?'

I thought you'd never ask.

'It was half a million pounds.'

Sister Hackett's eyes sparkled with something like glee.

'Oh, isn't that wonderful? She was here for eight years, committed by the magistrates for an assault on another woman who she said was persecuting her. Persecution mania. She responded well to treatment here, and over the years she became very much attached to what they call

Anglo-Catholicism. The local vicar would visit her — he was more Roman than Rome — and they'd have long chats together. We considered those visits highly therapeutic. She — well, perhaps I've said too much.'

Nurse Hackett bit her lip. *She's dying to hear the rest of my lies*, thought Chloe. *I mustn't keep her waiting.*

'Think what a difference that money could make for her, after all her years of suffering! Losing all her family — her sister's husband, baby Ellie, and then her sister too! This isn't just an investigation for us, Sister, it's more of a pilgrimage.'

Watch it! Don't go too far!

'Oh, you're so right. What did the great-uncle die of?'

'Die of? It was — it was lockjaw. Very unusual, I think.'

'Oh, yes, very, but it does happen. So as I say, she became very religious in a sensible sort of way, and when the first women priests were ordained, she became a real partisan in their cause. And all the time she was ridding herself of her obsessions, due to the marvellous psychiatric care she received here.'

'I'd love to present her with a cheque for half a million pounds.' Chloe sighed wistfully.

'I hope I can help you find her. When Melanie left here, she managed to secure the post of housekeeper to a very successful vicar somewhere in the south. I forget her name. I remember thinking how well matched they'd be, with Melanie having taken up the cudgels on their behalf!'

'Was Melanie completely cured when she left here?'

Sister Hackett looked surprised.

'We don't really use the term "cured" when it comes to mental illness. But she was deemed no longer a threat to the general public, as long as she took her medication and continued to use the coping skills she learnt here — and she would have had aftercare at her local NHS for as long as she needed it. She wasn't a voluntary patient, you see. She was here under restraint.'

'You've been so kind, Sister Hackett,' said Chloe. 'It's always a pleasure to speak to a true professional.'

Sister Hackett blushed with pleasure.

'It's very kind of you to say so, Mrs McArthur. Now let me get that address for you.'

Sister Hackett left her office, and was gone for so long that Chloe wondered whether she had relented her willingness to talk, and was fetching the security guards. But no. Sister Hackett returned with a cardboard folder, from which she extracted a handwritten letter. 'It's chaos in the records room at the moment,' she said. 'They're decorating, and all the filing cabinets have been shoved together in the corridor. Anyway, there's this letter that the vicar sent to Melanie, who'd written to her, asking for a job. It might help you find her.'

St John the Baptist Vicarage,
Calton Street,
Paddington.
21 March 2012

Dear Miss Grint,

Thank you so much for writing. It so happens that I am feeling the need for some domestic help at the moment, and would love to see you. Can you come next Thursday? If we find that we suit each other, we can discuss terms. I am very happy to hear that you are a supporter of women's ordination. As you obviously know, our ministry is still a bit of an uphill struggle.

I look forward to meeting you.
Yours sincerely,
Stacey Williams
Vicar

There came a sudden gasp of horror from Sister Hackett.

'*Stacey Williams*. Wasn't that the poor woman who was slaughtered at the altar? Poor Melanie! How will she cope with that?'

'Thank you for all your help, Sister,' said Chloe. 'When I find Melanie, I'll give her your regards.'

9. THE FELLOWSHIP OF CAPRICORN

'We let Melanie Grint slip off the radar,' said DS Edwards. 'After the murder of Stacey Williams she just upped sticks and disappeared.'

'Until now that didn't seem suspicious,' said Noel Greenspan. 'Everyone said she was devoted to Stacey. She'd been with her for, what, seven years? There was nothing to keep her at Rushbrooke Hill after the murder.'

'Now it seems that she had every reason to hold a grudge against her employer. I only spoke to her once,' said DI French. 'I wish I'd paid more attention to her when I went there. It was she who told me Stacey was terrified of Julian Stringer. Now I don't know if that's true.'

The four investigators had come together at Jubilee House in Oldminster to pool resources.

'I've interviewed Julian Stringer,' said Glyn Edwards, 'and there's no doubt in my mind that he needs psychiatric help. But I'm more and more convinced that he had nothing to do with the death of Stacey Williams. And I don't believe that he put that pig's blood in the font. He was appalled at the idea.'

'What are you suggesting?' asked DI French.

'I'm suggesting that we narrowed our focus to Julian Stringer too quickly, without questioning or interviewing anyone else in that village, Rushbrooke Hill. We brought the case away with us, if you see what I mean. Was there anything of significance that we left behind?'

'It's a thought,' said DI French. 'So far, we've established that there were a few people who may have held grudges against Stacey, some of them related to her choice of job and others related to the trail of deaths she left in her wake. Melanie Grint is the most obvious candidate, and she had plenty of opportunities to poison the wine. But we must build a strong case, and that involves questioning and ruling out other potential suspects. Maybe that's something that could interest you, Noel? After all, you're working for Colonel Calderdale, and the discreet presence of private detectives would be preferable to police officers descending on the village.'

'Chloe and I would be delighted to put our skills to the test in Rushbrooke Hill,' said Noel. 'I'll phone Calderdale myself today, and fix something up.'

'There's an element of madness in this case, of instability, if you like,' French went on thoughtfully. 'Melanie Grint had a history of mental trouble, and so did that rogue clergyman, Julian Stringer. And maybe there's a Mr X, someone quite unknown to us, who murdered Stacey Williams for personal reasons, reasons quite unconnected with bogies and demons and superstition.

'So we need to find Melanie, and question her further. She may have heard things, seen things, that made her flee from Rushbrooke Hill as soon as she could.'

'Sir,' said DS Edwards, 'isn't it obvious she fled *because she was guilty*? Stacey's actions led to the death of Melanie's brother-in-law; the mental torture must have affected her sister. Did Melanie work her way into Stacey's confidence in order to murder her when the opportunity presented itself?'

'And yet,' pointed out Chloe, 'she waited seven years to strike. Why? And why not choose a method that would give her an alibi?'

'When I interviewed Julian Stringer,' said DS Edwards, 'he said something very interesting to me. He'd been going on about Stacey being an energumen — a woman possessed by a demon — and then he said, "I know something about energumens, I've met them before." They were not his exact words, but I wondered at the time whether he was referring to Melanie. He was talking about the pig's blood in the font.'

* * *

Noel and Chloe decided to take a mini-break at Rushbrooke Hill, booking rooms at the Farmer's Arms, the local inn. The village was only a few miles from Oldminster, but they both felt that they needed to get the 'feel' of the place by staying there a while. There was a car park opposite the inn, where Noel was able to leave his battered Ford Mondeo.

Nigel Calderdale was very pleased to see them both, and hear of their latest findings when they called on him at Rushbrooke House, his beautifully furnished home in the village high street. They gave him an account of their enquiries into the earlier career of the Reverend Stacey Williams, including the string of domestic tragedies that she had left in her wake. The colonel was suitably impressed.

'So it could well have been someone from her past who came out here seeking revenge for some harm, real or imagined . . . Oh, dear! Why did I not behave like a sensible human being, and try to gain her confidence? She had no one close to confide in, except for that housekeeper, Melanie Grint. But it's too late, now, for me to make amends.'

'How are things here now, in Rushbrooke Hill?' asked Noel.

'I'd say that things are more or less back to normal. We've started to look for a new vicar, though I don't suppose there'll be a flood of applicants after what happened here. Oh, and now we've got a ghost!'

Nigel Calderdale gave a kind of amused sigh.

'There's an old man who's lived in the village all his life, a retired cobbler called Reuben Oldacre. He's well into his eighties, but quite hale and hearty, though I think there's the onset of something or other — Parkinson's, Alzheimer's, something like that. Very fond of the drink, is old Reuben. Well, a few nights ago he told his friends in the pub that he'd seen the ghost of Stacey Williams wandering around the churchyard. So any new vicar will have to put up with their predecessor looking over their shoulder!'

'Does this Rueben prop up the bar at the Farmer's Arms?' asked Noel. 'That's where we're staying.'

'Oh, no, the Farmer's Arms is too posh for Reuben. He spends his evenings in the Crown Vaults, an alehouse in Mab Lane, just beyond the old school buildings. But before you talk to him, why don't you go and have a word with Dr John Miller? He's our church organist as well as being the local doctor, and he's a fund of knowledge about the villagers and their doings. He's also a self-confessed gossip. He'd love to see you both.'

* * *

'Mr Greenspan? I rather think that you and I are brothers under the skin. We're both "falling into flesh", as they say, and haven't quite as much hair as we'd wish, though a glance in the mirror will show that we're both very distinguished men.'

Dr Miller had received them in his comfortable 1930s house. His surgery occupied the front room. His cosy living quarters in the rear of the house seemed to be a combination of dining room, study and library. There were books all over the place, an old television set, and a skull in a glass case on the mantelpiece.

'You're very kind, Doctor,' said Noel, entering into the bantering spirit of their host, 'and I must say that I was struck at once by your noble bearing. May I introduce my business partner, Mrs Chloe McArthur?'

'Enchanted. Take a seat, both of you. Chloe, chuck those magazines on the floor. We'll have some tea and Hobnobs in a minute. Now, how can I help you?'

'We've been delving into the past career of the Reverend Stacey Williams,' said Noel. 'I think you might know that we are employed by Colonel Nigel Calderdale, who thought that the police didn't ask enough questions locally about the vicar's murder. We were wondering whether you could give us some verbal portraits of the more interesting inhabitants of Rushbrooke Hill.'

'Potential murderers, you mean? Well, there's Phil Taylor, who runs the fishmonger's at the top of the high street. He's had a long-running feud with the newsagent over parking violations, and had been heard more than once to say that he'd swing for him one of these days, even though we don't have the death sentence anymore. But I don't think he'd have murdered the vicar. He's a Methodist, or so he says, and while they have their differences with the C of E, I don't think they run to murder.

'And then there's Mrs Adele Starkadder, our spiritualist medium. She also reads palms, and you can leave a donation in a bowl at the door as you go out. Her spirit guide is her late husband, Arthur, who fell under a train twenty years ago, having lost his footing on the edge of the platform at Shipley Halt.'

'And do you see her as a potential murderer?' asked Chloe.

'Not really. Adele's a kindly soul, who believes in her psychic powers. She has a little church in her back garden, a kind of wooden hut, where her followers — there's four of them — meet every Sunday. I went to listen, once. My grandfather came through to urge me to do as much good as I could to everyone. He must have changed once he got to the Other Side. In life, he was a cantankerous old cuss. Then Adele read us an extract from Silver Ghost — no, that was a Rolls Royce. *Silver Birch*, that's it. Very uplifting stuff, actually.'

'But could she have murdered the vicar?' Chloe persisted.

'Possibly, though I can't think how she could have contrived it. Stacey Williams came to visit Adele, you see, very soon after she got here. She'd signed a truce with the

Methodist minister, or whatever it is these clergy people do, and then it was Adele's turn. Stacey pulled no punches. She told her that séances were consorting with demons, and that spiritualism was all nonsense. She urged her to turn her back upon it, and come to church instead. By the time she'd finished, Adele knew where she stood with the Establishment.'

'How do you know all this?' asked Noel.

'Well, of course, Adele came to see me in floods of tears. I told her not to take any notice, and I prescribed some anti-depressants for her. Then we had a cup of tea, and then a drop of something stronger, and Adele began to cheer up. She may have murdered Stacey to get her revenge, but I very much doubt it.'

There it was again: that intransigence, that refusal to compromise, that had been a central aspect of Stacey's character. Convinced of her own righteousness, she was quite incapable of understanding the views of others. And yet in so many ways she had been a resounding success in her vocation.

'How about Reuben Oldacre?' asked Chloe.

'Reuben? Who told you about him? He's an old soak, more often drunk than not, and with more than enough money to indulge his hobby of drinking. But he wouldn't murder anybody, certainly not the vicar. On the rare occasions that he's sober, he mows the grass in the churchyard. You know he's seen Stacey's ghost? She wouldn't have liked that. What with her always being right, and murdered into the bargain, she'd have expected to go straight to heaven, not condemned to wandering around the churchyard in the depths of night. Goodness knows what else Reuben sees when he's in his cups. Anyway, he's not long for this world. I won't go into details, but old Reuben's time on earth is drawing to a close. Time for some refreshment. Excuse me for a minute.'

'Glyn Edwards was right,' said Chloe, when their host had left the room. 'There are all kinds of interesting eccentrics here in this village, none of whom were ever questioned or interviewed. I don't think any of these could have murdered Stacey, but you never know.'

Dr Miller returned with a tray containing three mugs of tea and a plate of biscuits. Chloe had a question she wanted to ask.

'Was Melanie Grint one of your patients?'

'No, or at least I never had an appointment with her. She may well have registered at the practice and never come in — that happens now and then. Or some people just don't bother to register with a GP at all — I think they must go to the walk-in clinic at Oldminster if they get sick. She was a very shy woman, but I liked her a lot, and she was devoted to poor Stacey. If anyone made a disparaging remark about her in her presence, then she lost her shyness, and told the person what she thought of them in no uncertain terms. And she was a marvellous cook, if like me you're fond of old-fashioned food. She used to cook great breakfasts for Stacey for when she returned from fasting Communion. Eggs and bacon, fried tomatoes and black puddings. I was fortunate to share one of those breakfasts. Marvellous! Oh, well, nobody knows where Melanie is, now.'

'You've been a mine of information, Doctor,' said Noel. 'Any more local eccentrics you'd care to tell us about?'

Dr Miller looked abashed.

'You'll have gathered that I'm a bit of a gossip, Noel, but one has to draw the line between gossip and slander. There *is* someone else, but by mentioning him I don't want you to think that I'm making any kind of accusation.

'About a mile from here, in Mosspit Lane, there's a run-down Tudor mansion which houses a sort of religious sect, called the Fellowship of Capricorn. Their leader is a man known as the Master of the Goat Herd, and he and his followers wear robes a bit like monks — but these folk are not monks. They go in for wholeness, mindfulness, spiritual awareness, conquering of Self. I've got a leaflet one of them gave me somewhere. They read Tarot cards and do Vedic chanting. Stuff like that. A lot of people round here think that they're Satanists.'

And the police didn't mention them to us! Chloe thought. *Inspector French packed his bags and decamped far too early. Glyn Edwards was right.*

'Did Stacey have any dealings with these people — the Fellowship of Capricorn?'

'Oh, yes, she went to warn them off, even though they'd been established there for years. There are about ten of them in residence, I believe. Tony Savidge, who is on the parish council, insisted on going with her, in case there was any funny business. Apparently it was a bit of an anti-climax. The Master of the Goat Herd listened patiently to Stacey's harangue, and then humbly suggested that there were many paths to Truth. Stacey had to be content with that, as it was clear that the man was not prepared to engage in arguments. She seemed satisfied, though. At least, she had made her presence known in the camp of one of her competitors.'

'A possibility, then,' said Noel. 'Maybe this Master of the Herd thought it would be a good idea to warn people off by getting rid of the vicar.'

'Maybe, but I very much doubt it. I don't know whether they're Satanists, but they seem a harmless bunch to me. Inspector French tells me they couldn't possibly have put blood in the font, anyway, as they were all away in the Cotswolds that night. They wear those fancy robes, but they look much the same as the rest of us when they're queuing with their wire baskets at the checkout in Stackpole's.'

* * *

'Noel,' said Chloe as they left Dr Miller's house, 'I'm minded to visit this Fellowship of Capricorn, and see whether I can wangle a membership. I'd like to practise the detective arts on the Chief Goat, to find out what his reactions were to Stacey's murder.'

'Well, if you do, I shall be parked outside, and if you're not out again in half an hour, I'll come in and rescue you. Dr Miller says they're harmless, but he may be wrong. And if you're going to pretend to join them, mention that you've a great deal of money — that's what lies behind all those mystery cults. And he's the Master of the Goat Herd, not the Chief Goat.'

'I'll take your advice,' said Chloe.

'Stacey Williams seems rather an intolerant type,' said Noel. 'You would think she would have been used to other religions after working in London. I wonder why she set about warning off the local spiritualists and pagans.'

'We've already seen she was lacking in compassion and open-mindedness. Perhaps she really did see them as devil worshippers? Or perhaps she thought they were charlatans preying on her flock,' replied Chloe. 'Now, I've been thinking about those black puddings Melanie Grint used to cook. She might well have made them herself or bought them at the supermarket, but I spotted a butcher's shop as we were coming here to see Dr Miller. A proper, old-fashioned butcher's, with trays of meat in the window, decorated with little sprigs of parsley — and strings of black puddings hanging from a rack.'

'Made on the premises by the butcher, would you say?'

'Decidedly.'

'But what does it matter where she got the black puddings?'

'Because they're made from pig's blood,' said Chloe. 'I bet you anything that butcher gets his blood from a local farmer. Worth a little investigation, I think.'

* * *

The Tudor manor house looked as though it had resigned itself to ongoing decay. The black-and-white timbers had faded to an indeterminate grey, and some of the windows had been boarded up. But Chloe was greeted cheerfully enough when her knock at the door brought a young man in a kind of smock decorated with moons and stars, who asked her what she wanted.

'I'd very much like to have an audience with the Master of the Goat Herd,' said Chloe. 'I've heard that he is a master of the esoteric mysteries. I have been a Rosicrucian for some time, but feel the need to progress beyond that.'

'This house is always open to enquirers,' said the young man, smiling. 'The master is free at the moment, so I can take you to him straight away.'

Chloe found herself in a dark panelled hall, lit by an array of dim coloured light bulbs. The walls had been crudely painted with figures of demons and spirits, evidently done by someone who liked defacing ancient panelling with crude daubs in acrylic paint. She looked at her guide. He was a fair-haired young man in his twenties, with pleasantly smiling eyes. She wondered what could have brought him to this peculiar place.

They reached the end of a corridor, and her guide knocked on a door, which was decorated with the skeleton of a bat. Whoever designed these things, thought Chloe, was a master of unsubtle contempt for the achievements of both the human and animal kingdoms.

When she entered the room, she saw nothing but the majestic figure sitting behind a vast carved desk. His aquiline features, his burning gaze, and his lion's mane of golden hair pulled back into a ponytail was a truly awesome sight. This was the Master of the Goat Herd, the ruler of the Fellowship of Capricorn, the man whom Stacey Williams had barracked, here in his den.

On the wall above the desk was the stuffed and mounted head of an enormous billy goat with curled horns, stiff beard, and staring glass eyes. Chloe shuddered, and averted her gaze. The Master of the Goat Herd smiled. When he spoke, there was nothing sinister about his voice, though his eyes continued to blaze with unseen fire.

'So, my dear lady,' he said, 'you have come here seeking spiritual guidance. I assume that, anyway. That's what most visitors seek when they come here. I'm sorry that Brother Kalon — the young man who brought you here — never thought to introduce you. He's well versed in the lesser esoteric doctrines, but not so well up in elementary manners. Sit down on that chair, and tell me what it is that you want.'

As the master spoke, the room seemed to be pervaded by a subtle perfume, and after a while a faint mist appeared to form around the master's head. Chloe could not take her eyes off those of the leonine practitioner of the occult arts.

'I have heard of you, Master,' said Chloe, 'and am curious as to what mysteries of the occult you are prepared to reveal to sincere enquirers. I am a wealthy woman, and I don't care what others think of what I do with my money. What I do with my own is nobody's business.' *That should do it.*

'Like all enquirers, you are obsessed with money and personal possessions.' The mist around the master's head seemed to increase. What was that perfume? She had encountered it before, but could not remember where. 'If you were to come here as a novice, you would have to tear your mind away from fantasies of wealth, and fill your mind with thought of the realities beyond reality.'

'I should so like to learn your doctrines,' said Chloe. 'My name is—'

The master held up a hand in warning.

'No names yet, my dear. It is too late for that. It you join us, you will be given a new name. Let me ask you a question. What kind of people do you think we are?'

'Sincere seekers after truth.'

'No. You know that is not the right answer. What kind of people do you think we are?'

'I think you might be Satanists.'

'And does that shock or frighten you?'

'No. I have heard of such people, and want to know more.'

'You might be a spy, sent here to worm your way into our confidence in order to destroy us. No, no, don't protest. You would not be the first to come here to betray us. But let that pass for the moment. Do you know the identity of the great goat whose likeness is fixed above me on the wall?'

'No.' *Thank goodness Noel was waiting outside.*

'It is a figure of the Goat of Mendes, one of the great servants of the Lord Satan. I am surprised that you do not know this, as you are allegedly seeking after the ancient truths. Have you heard of Eliphas Lévi?'

Chloe shook her head.

'You surprise me,' the master went on. 'There are certain ceremonies in which the Goat of Mendes appears to Satan's worshippers, and achieves its desires with the female members of his cult. So if you truly want to follow the esoteric doctrines, you will have to repudiate all the moral restrictions imposed upon mankind by the Abrahamic faiths, and yield yourself willingly to the Goat and his followers. Now you can see why we are called the Fellowship of Capricorn. *Capricornus* is the Latin word for "goat-horned".'

'And what powers would I receive in return?'

'You would be given the spirit of divination, and the power to hypnotise anyone to do your bidding. Were you to invest your money in certain bonds known to the fellowship, your capital would be returned a hundredfold.'

Suddenly, the Master of the Goat Herd rose up from his desk, and to Chloe he seemed to be something more than human.

'But those who betray us had better beware! Let me tell you the fate of one enemy who came here, bent on destroying me and my followers. She was a Christian priest, Stacey Williams, who stood where you are sitting now, and all but challenged me to a duel of faiths. I spoke civilly to her because she was accompanied by Tony Savidge, a local garage owner and a useful friend. But when they had gone, I consigned her to the God Baphomet.'

The room seemed to grow dark, and it was filled with a kind of choking sweetness. The master's eyes blazed, and those of the goat on the wall glowed red.

'I destroyed her by controlling her will from a distance. I overshadowed her mind and took her puny spirit captive. By the time I had finished she was little more than an automaton, totally subdued to my control. *And then I ordered her to kill herself.* She was our enemy, you see, an enemy of the Old Religion. Today, I have shown you something of the powers that you crave to exert. Go, now, and think about what I have told you. In exchange for knowledge, service will be required. Go.'

The mist dispersed, and the room returned to normal. The master seemed now to be what he had first seemed to be, a majestic, benign figure. But for all that, Chloe McArthur gasped in relief when she stood outside the Tudor house and saw Noel Greenspan waiting for her beside the car.

* * *

'Sit there, Chloe,' said Noel, 'and sip that gin and tonic while I debrief you. I'm not surprised that he scared you with his half-veiled threats and silly boasts. The Master of the Goat Herd is yet another charlatan with the gift of the gab and an eye on the main chance. He's living the life of Riley there, supported by his coterie of dupes who cough up the money when required, and in return enjoy being fooled by a first-rate confidence trickster. Notice how he suddenly switched off the mumbo jumbo to invite you to invest your money in a scheme that would make impossible returns. I'm minded to go back in there and throttle him.'

'I'd rather you didn't,' said Chloe. 'I'm feeling much better now, but he *was* an impressive figure. And there was a strange, mystic atmosphere in that room. There was almost a cloud around him — the goat's eyes really were glowing, Noel. I felt almost as if I was having a vision . . .'

'Now that's interesting. A little old-fashioned, mind you. He would have had a kind of console under that desk, from which he could operate the pumping of an hypnotic into the room — probably something derived from hemp, or from an hallucinatory drug like LSD or psilocybin. They can be diluted with water or alcohol and sprayed into the atmosphere. The glowing goat's eyes was a bit crude, but easily done with a rheostat switch.'

'You seem to know an awful lot about these things,' said Chloe.

'When I was a young man, working with Sidney Foster, one of the great London private detectives, I helped him expose a scam called the New Harvest, led by a man called the Reaper — another of these tin-pot messiahs. He was worse than your Chief Goat. He entrapped young girls with his promises of magic and virtually sold them into prostitution. More raper than reaper. He got twelve years without remission.'

'What about my Chief Goat's claims that he hypnotised Stacey into killing herself?'

'That was a very dangerous boast for him to make, but he couldn't resist scaring you. Stacey Williams seems to have been a strong-willed, determined woman, who couldn't have been hypnotised by anyone. And as you know, a person under hypnotic influence can't be made to act against their nature. Suicide? I think not.

'But I don't like the sound of our Master of the Goat Herd. I'm going to ask DI French to make a few enquiries. This man might be something more dangerous than a spiritual fraudster.'

'What shall we do next?'

'I have a whole programme of local activities in mind, Chloe, but first, let's have a sustaining pub lunch here, at the Farmer's Arms. We need to fortify the inner man.'

'And woman?'

'Well, yes. Maybe they do an all-day breakfast, complete with black puddings.'

10. THE BIN BAGS AND OTHER MATTERS

Hinton's Farm lay at the end of a winding lane on the northern limit of the village. It was a more extensive place than Noel Greenspan had imagined, with a number of farm buildings grouped around a yard on which stood a tractor and a couple of well-used SUVs. Mr Hinton was happy to talk. He was a strongly built, sun-bronzed man in his forties.

'Yes, I have pigs and sheep here, as well as a couple of fields under arable. The sheep are reared for market, but the pigs are bred for bacon, and I do my own slaughtering.'

'And you make black puddings, I believe.'

'Yes. I sell them direct from here, and I also supply the village butcher. People come here from miles around to buy my home-cured bacon, sausages and black puddings.'

'Did Miss Grint buy from you?'

'Yes, she did. I thought I was going to have a regular customer with her, but then the vicar was murdered, and Miss Grint sheared off somewhere. You're detectives, aren't you? The word's going round that you're here to solve the mystery of who done the vicar in. Terrible, that was.'

'Could anyone have stolen some of the blood you use for the black puddings?'

'You're thinking of that business with the font. Diabolical, that was. I was christened in that font, and so was our Alice and our Tom. Come over here, across the yard, and I'll show you.'

Noel and Chloe followed Mr Hinton until they came to a detached shed. The farmer undid the padlock and they entered a space almost filled with three great stainless steel vats. There was a strong smell of blood in the air.

'You see these vats? This is where the pig's blood is stored under the required temperature and conditions. They're empty for cleaning at the moment.'

He opened the lid of one of the vats.

'Easily opened, you see. Anyone could have come here with a jug and scooped up enough blood to fill that glass bowl in the font. The day it all happened I found the lid here loose and blood spilt on the ground. The police have seen all this. I never kept this place locked. Who'd expect some damn vampire to come sniffing around? After that happened, I put a hasp and staple on the door, and bought a good strong padlock. We're all church folk in this family, and well — that business of blood in the font, that was really evil. Only a twisted mind could think of doing a thing like that.'

'It could have been Melanie,' said Noel, after they had left the farm. 'She could have gone there to buy some bacon and black puddings, and while she was on the premises have nipped into that shed and filled a screw-cap bottle with blood. Something like that.'

'Exactly,' said Chloe. 'My money's on her for the murderer. She's done a runner and Stacey was implicated in her brother-in-law's death. I don't buy all this talk about her being devoted to Stacey.'

'Hm . . . Well, we'll see. It's only half past eleven. How about an unannounced call on the local medium? What was her name? Mrs Adele Starkadder.'

* * *

'Word soon got round that there were detectives in the village,' said Adele Starkadder. 'I wondered whether you'd come knocking at my door.'

Mrs Starkadder, a pleasant, cheerful woman in her sixties, was not a bit what Chloe had expected. No diaphanous garments, clanking beads and scarabs. She was wearing a floral dress and a string of pearls. Her cottage was well furnished with what Chloe judged to be genuine antiques. There were vases of seasonal flowers on the window sills.

'I believe that the Reverend Stacey came here to lay her cards on the table,' said Noel.

'She did, she did!' The medium gave a good-humoured laugh. 'She told me that I was consorting with demons, and that I should give up the vocation of a lifetime and come to church every Sunday. I told her that I was very happy to come to church, if that would please her, and I think she was rather taken aback by that. We treated each other with cold civility, and I never saw her again. Not to speak to, anyway.'

'And you didn't murder her?' asked Noel.

Adele Starkadder laughed. 'My, you are direct, aren't you? No, I didn't murder her. As far as I could tell, she was a good, decent woman, though rather narrow-minded. But there are wicked people around here. I'm referring to the Fellowship of Capricorn. They're evil, because they want to deceive, and to overcome goodness with badness. That man, the Master of the Goat Herd — you should exercise some of your skills in delving into his past.'

'Did you ever come across the Reverend Julian Stringer?'

'Yes, I saw him once, sermonising to a little crowd at the village cross — ranting and raving, to my mind. He was rather rude about the Reverend Stacey, and one of the men threatened to knock him down if he didn't move on. There was nothing very reverend about *him*, I can tell you. I think the poor, silly man was mad.'

'Old Reuben Oldacre saw a ghost in the churchyard,' said Chloe. 'Have you seen it, perhaps? Ghosts being in your line of business, so to speak.'

Again, the good-humoured laugh.

'I asked him about that, you know, and he said that the ghost was wearing a white dress down to her ankles, and moved without a sound. Well, that told me everything. There's a young lady living not far from the church with her cantankerous old father, who won't let her see any young men in case she fancies one of them, and gets married. He wouldn't have a skivvy to look after him, then.

'She's fallen in love with a certain young man who lives on the far side of the village, and there are times when she leaves the house after her father's gone to sleep and flits across the churchyard to see her young man. She wears her nightdress, with a long, white dressing gown, which made her look like a ghost to old Reuben. He'd no right to be out after midnight.'

'How do you know what she wears on her midnight trips?' asked Noel.

'I know because I've seen her myself. Not in a trance, but as a result of watching out for her. The advantage of being a widow is that you can go out at night without anyone wanting to know where you're going.'

Adele Starkadder held her head in her hands for a moment, and then gave a little shudder. For one anxious moment Chloe thought she was about to go into a trance.

'Very pleased to have met you both,' she said as she accompanied them to the door. 'And Chloe, does the name Pietermaritzburg mean anything to you? Yes, I see it does. Well, don't worry about Alex. It's not a stroke.'

As they walked down the path to the road, Chloe McArthur took Noel's arm to steady herself. 'Oh, Noel,' she whispered, 'how could she have known about my Uncle Alex? I only received a text about him collapsing late last night.'

'I don't know how she knew,' said Noel, 'and I didn't know you had an Uncle Alex. Maybe she heard something on the spiritualists' grape vine. Is your uncle an Oldminster man?'

'No, he's lived in South Africa for over thirty years. In Pietermaritzburg.'

'Among this cast of fakes, frauds and fanatics, maybe we've just been speaking to the genuine article.'

* * *

Rushbrooke vicarage felt desolate and abandoned. Most of the furniture had been removed by Stacey's parents, and the walls showed discoloured squares and rectangles where pictures had once hung.

'She wasn't here long enough to have the rooms redecorated,' said Nigel Calderdale. 'Her predecessor, old Canon Harper, was content with a kind of dim and faded clutter.'

Noel and Chloe walked from room to room, their footsteps echoing in the empty abandoned house. It had been Noel's idea to 'look around', and Colonel Calderdale, who held the vicarage keys, had joined them. They went upstairs, and examined the three bedrooms. The main room was entirely bare of any furnishings. That, thought Chloe, would have been Stacey's bedroom. A second bedroom had an old-fashioned iron bedstead with a bare mattress laid on it. This had probably been Melanie's room. The third room was quite empty, and looked as though it had never been used. It contained a steel filing cabinet, all the drawers of which were open and empty. There was a bathroom at the end of the upstairs corridor. Again, nothing of interest was to be found there.

They went downstairs into the kitchen. A smell of stale food still lingered in the room. Calderdale used a key to open the back door, and they stepped out into a yard, beyond which stretched the rear garden. Three black bin bags rested on top of a blue wheelie bin near the back gate, which was bolted.

The two detectives looked at each other. The looks said: here is something right up our street.

'Colonel,' said Noel, 'Mrs McArthur and I would like to stay here for a while and take a closer look. Could you let us have the keys? When we're done here, we'll bring them straight back to you at Rushbrooke House.'

When the colonel had gone, they set about their work. They put the three bin bags down on the yard, and examined the contents of the blue wheelie bin. It contained a number of flattened cardboard boxes that had once held cornflakes, a few soup tins, all carefully swilled before being thrown away, three empty wine bottles, and piles of old newspapers and magazines, including back numbers of the *Oldminster Gazette*, and a bundle of *Radio Times* secured with string. Mixed in with all this was the usual junk mail, and a few loose copies of the *Daily Telegraph* and the *Daily Mirror*.

'Would it be elitist of me to suggest that the *Telegraph*s were Stacey's, and the *Mirror*s Melanie's?' said Chloe.

'Not elitist, just snobbish. But yes, I think you're right. The most interesting point is that these things were never put out for collection, because there was suddenly no one in the vicarage to do so, and the refuse collectors couldn't get into the yard because the gate's bolted on the inside. Let's look at the dates on these papers — yes, they're all before Stacey was murdered. Deduction, please, Mrs McArthur.'

'Stacey and Melanie kept a pile of old newspapers and magazines in the house until they were ready to dump them in the yard. When the bin was full, they filled some bin bags, and placed them on top of the bin. No, that's not quite accurate. I think it's most likely that *Melanie* filled those bags after Stacey was murdered. We know that she'd no intention of staying, and as we saw, the house itself seems to have been stripped bare. Let's open the bin bags.'

The first bag contained a set of musty old curtains and what Chloe said was a good quality woman's formal dress, which seemed to have been torn or slashed with a knife. There were also three pairs of shoes which had obviously belonged to Stacey. Evidently, they had been of no use to Melanie Grint.

The second bag contained a clerical cassock which had also been torn and slashed, and two books: a Bible and a very handsome copy of the *Book of Common Prayer*. Inscriptions on the fly-leaves showed that they had both belonged to the Reverend Stacey Williams. Chloe handed the two books to Noel, who examined them in silence for a while, flicking through the pages.

'"For Stacey, from Mummy and Daddy", it says in the Bible. And in this prayer book the inscription reads: "To the

Reverend Stacey Williams, on the occasion of her ordination to the priesthood. Richard Chartres, Bishop of London".'

Noel Greenspan put the two books on top of the blue wheelie bin.

'I don't like this, Chloe,' he said. 'Stacey must surely have valued these books. Why have they been thrown out with the trash? There's something . . . No, it's gone. I'm going to take these books, Chloe, and post them to Stacey's parents. I'll let Paul French know what I've done.'

'I don't like it, either, Noel. And I don't like that slashed dress, and the torn cassock. Julian Stringer was still at large when these things were put here. Perhaps this was his doing. We'd better open this third bag. I shudder to think what we'll find in it.'

It appeared to be full of bank statements dating back twenty years, and all belonging to Canon Harper. Evidently the old clergyman had left pockets of neglected possessions in various corners of the vicarage, and either Stacey or Melanie had thought it was time to get rid of them. There were three bulky and out-of-date telephone directories, and a pile of shredded paper. Underneath all of this were three letters, minus envelopes, torn across and discarded.

At this point, it started to rain.

'Chloe,' said Noel, 'you take these and the two books back to the Farmer's Arms, where we can examine them at leisure. I'll take the keys back to the colonel, and join you straight away.'

When Noel returned to the inn, they sat in his bedroom and examined the torn-across letters. They were all personal, and addressed to Stacey Williams. One, from an address in Worcester, was from an old school friend, with news that one of their former classmates had just married a man who owned a string of shops, and wasn't it marvellous? A second letter was from a young clergyman who had been ordained at the same time as Stacey, giving her news of two old friends who had just been appointed to very desirable parishes. The third—

'Oh, look at this, Noel! You'd better read this!'

The Beeches,
Spinney Road,
Prior's Ford,
Hampshire.
4 March 2018

Dear Miss Williams,
My wife and I have decided to accept your assurance that nothing improper happened between you and Gregory. We have decided to do so because of the marvellous work you have done in this parish for the last three years, but I must say at once that we still have grave doubts about your behaviour to our son, who is only seventeen. We both urge you to regard your work here in Prior's Ford as done, and that you actively seek another living far from here.
Yours faithfully,
John Standish

'Another scandal! It's a daunting scenario that there may be a whole string of avengers across the whole country who suffered in one way or another from Stacey's administrations. What did you think of those three letters, I mean as a detective?'

'I felt that they were there for the police to find — two harmless letters and one full of dynamite. But the police never bothered to examine the vicarage. They took the case with them back to Oldminster, as Glyn Edwards said. Well, it's never too late. Once Paul French has seen that letter, he'll very quickly dig up the dirt for us.'

* * *

'That letter told it all,' said Detective Inspector French. 'I wonder why she kept it? Most people would want to burn a letter like that, or shred it. Perhaps she kept it as a kind of penance — something to look at when she was feeling too proud of her achievements. But it's odd the way it turned up, neatly torn across, in that bin bag. And the back gate was locked, you say? It looks as though our mystery man or woman banked on the police going through everything in the vicarage, but we didn't, so the planted evidence of Stacey's indiscretion — for I think that's what it was, you know — planted — was never seen by us. And Mr X couldn't risk going back to retrieve it. But why plant it at all? Poor Stacey was dead by then, presumably.'

'Stacey's enemies would stop at nothing to besmirch her character, even after she was dead,' said Chloe. 'Mr X wanted us to hear about what could have been a juicy scandal, but which was hushed up. She was very lucky there. Most parents wouldn't have connived with the seduction of a minor, which is what this was.'

'Well,' said DI French, 'it was yet another sad tale of woe. I got the details from someone I know in the Hampshire Constabulary. This lad, Gregory Standish, was an altar server at the church in Prior's Ford, and had grown very fond of Stacey, who once again had turned a moribund parish round. And then one day someone caught them kissing in the vestry. Gregory was only seventeen, and still at school. The person who caught them went straight away and told the parents. Why he didn't call the police, I don't know. They didn't want any scandal, and their son was adamant that he had kissed her, without her consent. They agreed to let the matter drop, as the letter showed us.

'They should have reported it. Although Gregory was over the age of consent, as a vicar Stacey was legally a "person of trust", which means any sexual activity with an under-eighteen in her care would have been a criminal act. It's quite incredible to me that these parents actually said in that letter that they didn't believe her protestations of innocence, and they did nothing. She herself denied that there had been any wrongdoing, which was a palpable lie.'

'Do we know that for certain?' asked Noel.

'Yes. Glyn went down to Hampshire and interviewed the man who had seen them kissing. Glyn told me that the man had obviously no personal axe to grind. He was just a decent man who knew right from wrong.'

'But,' pointed out Chloe, 'that doesn't prove anything, does it? This witness saw them kissing but he didn't see who kissed who, or if Stacey was trying to push him away. If the boy himself said he forced himself on her—'

'He might have been covering up for her when he said that.'

Chloe groaned. 'It's like her Cambridge "romance" all over again — rumour and scandal, but without interviewing the other party or Stacey herself we don't know what happened. Why on earth didn't Glyn interview Gregory Standish? He must be old enough to—'

'That's just it; he isn't. It was another tragedy in the wake of the Reverend Stacey Williams.'

'Tragedy?'

'Yes, Gregory Standish went off the rails after Stacey left, and got in with the wrong crowd. He died of a drug overdose in a nightclub just a week before his eighteenth birthday.'

* * *

'Well, Miss Patmore, I hope you've enjoyed your stay in West Deering. Your taxi will be here at twelve o'clock.'

Mrs Welby had warmed to Miss Patmore during her stay in her B & B. She had been a very tidy and helpful guest, secretary to a lawyer somewhere in London, and needing a rest after an operation.

'It's been a welcome break, Mrs Welby, and there are some lovely walks round here. I'll leave my case in the hall, and have another walk near that abbey or whatever it is.'

'Holy Cross Abbey,' said Mrs Welby. 'It's a kind of nursing home. It's been there for years, and the man in charge, the Abbot, is a very nice man. They make honey and jam there, all kinds of things.'

'I'll go out now and walk down there. It's a pity the grounds aren't open to the public.'

'As a matter of fact,' said Mrs Welby, 'if you turn right as you approach the abbey, you'll see a little lane — more of a track — that'll lead you to an iron kissing gate, which will take you into what they call the meadow. It's out of sight of the house, and there's some kind of shrine or grotto there, though it's all broken down, I believe.'

Mrs Welby laughed. 'Although the monks don't know it, their meadow is a kind of lovers' lane, used by the local lads and their girlfriends. So no one's going to notice if you go for a walk there. The lovers don't come out till evening!'

* * *

The Reverend Julian Stringer walked through the grounds of Holy Cross Abbey, mulling over what Dr Weinreb had told him. 'You need specialist psychiatric care, Mr Stringer, something that we can't give you here. A month in the Oldminster Special Unit should see you restored to something like your old self.'

Something like your old self.

He would conduct his battle against the energumens to the end, but there was no doubt that his daily sessions with Dr Weinreb had made him more settled in his mind. He had learnt to control his tongue, and tame his desire to preach openly to people who were not prepared to listen.

He was due to leave the abbey for the special psychiatric unit at the beginning of next week, and was in some ways looking forward to the experience. Now that people were finding his behaviour more acceptable, maybe they would listen to what he could tell them about the events at Holy Trinity, Rushbrooke Hill. The time had come to stop ranting, and tell these good doctors all that he knew about the pig's blood in the font.

He left the grounds, and strolled into the meadow. There was a Lourdes grotto built in a clump of lime trees, a curious thing to find in a Church of England establishment. But the abbey had once been a Roman Catholic convent, and when the nuns moved to a new home in the 1970s, they had left the grotto behind them. It had long been neglected, but it was a quiet spot where one could meditate in peace. After all, the Virgin Mary was destined to bruise Satan's heel, if the Scriptures were to be believed.

Someone had got there before him, a lady in a tweed coat and a bobble hat. Oh, well, it would be someone different to talk to. He walked towards the grotto, and as he got nearer, he realised who the woman was.

* * *

'Detective Sergeant Edwards? Abbot Richardson here. There's a police constable here from West Deering, and he's down in the meadow, but I wanted you to know what's happened before the news breaks.'

'And what *has* happened, Abbot?'

'It's Julian Stringer. Somebody's stabbed him in the back. I'm afraid he's dead.'

* * *

The Reverend Julian Stringer had fallen forward, and lay with his arms flung out above his head. The area around the ruined grotto had been secured with blue and white tape. Dr Raymond Turner saw how the SOCO officers in their white bodysuits were examining the grass of the meadow, working in a sort of arc across to the main abbey buildings. Later, they would sweep the grounds in the opposite direction.

DI French joined him, and asked his familiar question.

'What have you got for me, Ray?'

'This man had been in a face-to-face conversation with someone, and then had turned away from whoever it was, and, as those footprints in the grass show, was beginning to walk away — walk, not run. A fairly intelligent guess would suggest that he had encountered someone here, someone he knew, perhaps, or who he felt was no threat, and after talking to them, turned away to return to the abbey. That's when the other person stabbed him in the back. Death would have been quick — possibly immediate. The position of the arms, showing that he made no attempt to break his fall, suggests that he was dead before he hit the ground.'

'Murder, then.'

'Oh yes, decidedly murder. You can see traces of footprints *here*, where the killer turned round and made his way across *there*, to the other side of the meadow. Not my field of expertise, and SOCO will give you the finer detail when they're done.' He paused for a moment and then said, 'Who'd want to murder a clergyman?'

'This man here was no ordinary clergyman. He was a mentally unhinged fanatic. Well, he's gone to his reward, if that's the right way of putting it, poor chap.'

They both saw DS Edwards coming across to them from the abbey buildings.

'Everyone in the abbey's accounted for,' he told them. 'This was almost certainly the work of an intruder. Stringer wasn't a very nice man, but I'm sorry he's dead. There's nothing worse than mental trouble, and he had plenty of that. It looks as though someone from his murky past finally caught up with him.'

By midday, the preliminary investigation was complete. SOCO had established that the murderer had gained entrance from a kissing gate in a remote corner of the grounds. No discarded weapon was found, either in the abbey grounds or in the village beyond. Julian Stringer's body was taken away by police ambulance to the mortuary in Oldminster.

In the afternoon the police went door-to-door in West Deering and learnt from Mrs Welby about her paying guest, Miss Patmore. She had been a quiet, tidy sort of woman, who had been recuperating from an operation. There had been a TV in her room, but she never bothered with it. Miss Patmore had shown curiosity about the abbey grounds, and she had told her how she could get in to them through the back gate beyond the meadow.

No, Miss Patmore had not booked in advance, but had simply turned up one morning and asked whether there was a room to let. She had very kindly paid cash in advance. Yes, she did mention that she came from London, but volunteered nothing further, and she, Mrs Welby, didn't ask her any questions. It was not her place to be too nosy about the private life of a paying guest. One thing was certain, though: that nice, quiet woman could have had nothing to do with the murder of that poor mad clergyman at the abbey.

* * *

'He was stabbed in the back with something like a steak knife,' said Dr Raymond Turner. A friendly soul, he had called in person at Jubilee House to tell French and Edwards the results of the post-mortem. 'Whether by accident or design, the killer struck a vital organ. The poor man would have died immediately. When I opened him up, I found no sign of any morbid conditions, and both his heart and lungs were sound. For his age, he was in very good health.'

'How about his brain?' asked DI French. 'Any signs of madness there?'

Ray Turner sighed. 'How on earth should I know? There was nothing obviously abnormal, so you can rule out things like advanced Alzheimer's, I suppose. Surely you'd need to talk to his psychiatrist or look at his medical records to find out about any mental illness? My task was to determine the cause of death, which I did.'

'Have I offended you? If so, I'm sorry.'

'No, no, I'm not offended, Paul. It's just that I'm not like those hard-bitten medical examiners on TV who never bat an eyelid when presented with a corpse. The people I dissect are just that to me, *people*. Nobody deserves to be stabbed in the back.'

11. THE HEADLESS STOCKBROKER

'I thought it was about time,' said Lance Middleton, 'for me to play host for a change, and entertain you two to dinner here, at the Savoy Grill. Don't you admire the exquisite décor, the impeccable service, the delicious food that for once you, Chloe, can simply enjoy without having first slaved for hours over your gas-fired Aga?'

'It's just marvellous,' said Chloe McArthur. 'And that bijou hotel near Lincoln's Inn — how did you discover that? It's so kind of you to put us up there for a week, Lance. Are we going to make Colonel Calderdale pay for all this?'

'No, this is on me. I may as well be frank with you. I've just emerged triumphant from a Chancery trial where my client was declared the sole heir of a defunct European banker, and was so pleased with the result that he doubled my fee. Hence my present bounteous generosity.'

Lance and Chloe had chosen the Savoy's renowned Dover sole meunière, while Noel Greenspan had succumbed to the forty-two-day dry-aged belted Galloway beef. When it came to wine, Lance simply asked the waiter to bring what he thought best for each course, something which very obviously caused the man great pleasure.

'You can get anything here,' said Lance. 'All the classical French stuff, and more experimental things. They do a proper Porterhouse steak for two, the type of thing Lord Peter Wimsey would share with his chums. You can get lobster Thermidor, and native rock oysters. This is the kind of thing that the righteous will be served in heaven.'

Noel watched his host as he chattered on about food, and could sense that there was something very serious lurking behind his bonhomie. In his typical fashion, Lance had not told them why he had invited them to stay for a week in London, but no doubt after they had returned to his cosy furnished chambers in Lincoln's Inn, he would tell them what it was all about.

They had begun dinner at seven. They left the Savoy at ten thirty, and all but fell into a taxi which took them to Lincoln's Inn Fields.

'We'll part here for the night,' said Lance, 'because we're all three of us sleepy as a result of all that food and wine. Wasn't the coffee good, too? Not just an afterthought, but a creation in its own right. Your snug hotel is just around the corner, over *there*. Kindly present yourself at my chambers not too early tomorrow morning, when all will be revealed. Good night.'

* * *

Next morning heralded what was to be a bright, warm day. Noel and Chloe presented themselves at Lance's chambers in Lincoln's Inn at ten o'clock. They were both familiar with the panelled set of rooms, with its bookshelves full of legal tomes, Lance's antique desk, the death masks on the wall, and his counsel's wig on its stand. It was a comfortable sanctuary for their bachelor friend.

They found Lance in sober mood, with no signs of his usual skittishness and mock pomposity. He looked distracted, as though something heavy was burdening him.

They sat down on his leather couch. He remained behind his desk, as though about to talk with a client. He seemed disinclined to speak, so Noel broke the silence.

'What's this all about, Lance?'

'It's about the Reverend Stacey Williams,' he said. 'She lies there in Kensal Green Cemetery, unavenged by God or man. Theologically, I suppose, Stacey's in heaven, but I can sense her presence more and more, here, in these chambers, but also in court. I felt she was there with us last night at the Savoy, pleading for justice. And she's saying—'

Lance broke off, and sat for a while absorbed in his own musings.

This is not like him, Chloe thought. *Has he allowed himself to become obsessed with Stacey? Why has he brought us here?*

'And she's saying that we're all looking at alternatives to the obvious. So let us now examine the obvious. I'm going to ask you a rather bold question: who is the most obvious suspect in Stacey's murder? Chloe, what do you think?'

'To me, it is obvious she was murdered by Melanie Grint. She had a motive: vengeance for the death of her sister's husband, and the sorrow Stacey caused her sister over her baby's death and burial. And she had the opportunity: she was in charge of the altar wine and was the person to pour it into the chalice. But I've no proof. I've been hunting for the means: where did she get the cyanide from? I'm sure the answer to that final question will give me the proof I need.'

'Noel. What do *you* think?'

'I'm very much inclined to agree with Chloe. When we searched the vicarage at Rushbrooke Hill we found a letter, left there very conveniently for the police to find, which implicated Stacey Williams in yet another scandal. What was the point of leaving that letter for the police to find? After all, Stacey was *dead*, and beyond any further harm.'

'I would suggest,' said Lance, 'that it was put there because the one who killed Stacey hated her so much that she was intent on blackening her character even though she was dead. She intended to pursue her victim beyond the grave.

You notice I say "she", because I agree with you both that Melanie Grint is the killer in this case.'

'I disagree, Lance,' Chloe said. 'I think it was put there to distract the police from the true killer. To put a scandal in their way, as it were, but the wrong scandal.'

'It might have been either — hatred or cunning. Another point in favour of our choice,' said Noel, 'is the fact that Melanie — it could only have been Melanie — threw Stacey's previous Bible and prayer book into the rubbish, instead of making sure that they were sent to her parents. That was an act motivated by *hatred*. She hid that hatred behind a mask of loyalty.'

'I've asked you to come to London for a particular purpose,' said Lance, 'which I'll tell you in a moment. But first, now that we all agree that Melanie Grint was the killer, how do you think she did it?'

'She was the sacristan,' said Chloe.

'Yes, she was, so what happened to her predecessor, the person in charge of the vestries when old Canon Harper was vicar? I contacted your client Colonel Nigel Calderdale, who told me that the previous sacristan was a very old man, who didn't want to carry on once Canon Harper had retired.'

'Leaving Melanie to step into the old man's shoes,' said Noel. 'Did Colonel Calderdale tell you that she had definitely assumed the role?'

'He did. He sounded very vexed about it, too. "It's going too far," he said, "these women are taking over the whole church." And then he had the grace to laugh at himself. However misguided he may have been, he's evidently come to his senses. So, yes, Melanie Grint was officially the sacristan.'

'She had her victim totally in her power,' said Chloe. 'She was in charge of the upkeep of the vicarage, and also in charge of the sacristy. So there was no changing of wine bottles. Melanie could have contaminated the bottle of Communion wine at any time before the service, and when it was time to fill the cruets, she could do so quite openly.

She knew, of course, that no one else would be harmed, as the chalice would have fallen on to the altar or on to the sanctuary steps before the Communion time had arrived for the congregation. She could dispose of the poisoned wine bottle later at leisure.'

'And that business of pig's blood in the font,' said Noel. 'That must have been Melanie, too, another act of cold hatred, like binning those sacred books. We know that Melanie bought bacon and other stuff from Hinton's farm, and she could have taken a bottle with her to purloin some of the pig's blood in that farm shed. So what's next, Lance? What are we going to do?'

'Well, first, I want to play you a recording of an interview with Linda Jefford, aged thirteen. Her mother contacted Paul French, and this is the resulting account.'

'And what's so special about Linda Jefford, aged thirteen?' asked Noel.

'Linda was one of the two servers on that terrible day,' said Lance. 'And she *saw* Melanie put that poison in the wine bottle.'

'A witness!'

Lance picked up his iPhone, fiddled about it with until he had the right file set up, and pressed play.

'No, sir,' came a reedy voice from the device, 'she couldn't see me, because I was in the sacristy, which is the room next door to the vestry. But I could see her. Not that I was looking for anything, mind, but I thought at the time it was a funny thing to do. I just thought it must be something that I hadn't learnt about yet.'

They recognised French's voice next. 'So what was it that she did, Linda? Just tell me in your own words.'

'She took the bottle of altar wine from the cupboard, and unscrewed it. When you see wine on telly, they always have corks which have to be pulled out with a thing, and then they spray the wine all over each other. Mum says that it's a wicked waste, when there's people dying of thirst all over the world.'

'Yes, Linda. So tell me what it was that Miss Grint did.'

'She opened the bottle, and then poured some of it down the sink by the big vestment chest. Then she took a little bottle — like a medicine bottle, it was — from her pocket, and poured some liquid into the wine bottle. She held a hanky to her nose, which made me think she had a cold. After that, she filled the glass cruet from the wine bottle, screwed the lid back on it, and then put it back in the cupboard. I came in, then, and Miss Grint asked me to fill the other cruet with water, and take them through into the sanctuary. So I did, and I put the tray with the cruets down on the credence table. And when the Reverend Stacey drank the wine, she died.'

They heard the girl sobbing, and a woman's voice saying, 'That's enough now, love. Surely you have everything you need, Inspector?'

Lance switched off his phone, and put it back into his pocket.

'So there you are,' he said. 'That's all the proof we need. Linda's account confirms our suspicion that the killer was Melanie Grint.'

He glanced at his watch.

'Let us begin the tracking down of our killer.'

* * *

'Where are you taking us?' asked Chloe. Lance had driven them far away from the West End to the thronging dockside area of Wapping, then across Tower Bridge into a complex of docks and repair basins. He was clearly well acquainted with this part of London, and drove with confidence, keeping the Thames in sight to their left until he came to Cherry Garden Pier in Rotherhithe, where he brought the car to a halt in front of a small factory.

'I've been taking you here,' said Lance. 'This is the first stop on our forensic pilgrimage. Thomas Perry and Sons, manufacturer of all things plastic — plastic bowls, plastic shelves, plastic panels — anything plastic, my friends, can be obtained from Thomas Perry and Sons. Wholesale only, of course. Shall we go in now, or would you prefer a mid-morning snack first? Good. There's a little place where I had something to eat when I was investigating that business of the Jamaica Road phantom — as I recall, it's only a stone's throw from the factory.'

He led them to a small dockside café, empty at that time of morning. It contained a few tables covered with plastic table cloths, each table furnished with a pepper and salt shaker and a large plastic tomato containing ketchup.

'What'll it be?' asked a young man who come from an inner room to serve them.

'Shall I order?' asked Lance. 'We'd like some of your splendid bacon sandwiches, and three mugs of proper London tea.' As the man went to get their order, Lance added, 'You'd be surprised what good things you can get in some of these little cafés. After this, we'll call on "the Prof", as they call him, the quality control chemist at Thomas Perry and Sons.'

* * *

The Prof was a cheerful young man in his thirties, the proud possessor of a head of flaming red hair. He received his visitors in a chemical laboratory reached by a flight of stairs from the ground floor of the works. It contained a large window from which you could look down on various machines, tended by a crew of men and women in protective overalls and wearing masks.

'They call me "the Prof" here,' said the young man, 'because I'm supposed to be clever. My real name's Geoff Halliday. So how can I help you?'

'As Mr Perry probably told you, I am a QC engaged in certain investigations in conjunction with the police and others. Mr Greenspan here, and Mrs McArthur, are private detectives. I've been spending some time identifying businesses that employ hydrocyanic acid in their manufacturing processes,' said Lance, 'particularly firms with premises on this side of the Thames in Bermondsey or Rotherhithe.'

'Yes, we have it on site. Hydrocyanic acid is used to produce various industrial chemicals such as methyl methacrylate, which is used in the manufacture of plastics and polymers. We have our own conversion plant here, though occasionally we buy in from other suppliers.'

'The hydrocyanic acid is very dangerous, isn't it?' asked Lance. He already knew the answer, but wanted to hear it confirmed by a specialist.

'Indeed it is — it's better known as cyanide. You can become very sick just by breathing the fumes. If you drink it, then death is certain — usually immediate.'

'Do you have any samples of hydrocyanic acid here, in your laboratory?'

'Yes, over here, in this rack, you can see two five hundred mil bottles of the stuff. Notice the warning labels. *Deadly poison. Do not touch without written authority.* The written authority is a note signed by me.'

The young chemist paused for a moment, eying the three investigators speculatively. Then he spoke.

'All this talk of hydrocyanic acid — someone's been telling you about Joe Patmore, haven't they?'

Lance Middleton permitted himself an ecstatic sigh.

'Ah! At last!' He turned to Noel. 'We progress. I was hoping for something like this. You perceive the connection?'

'I'm not sure—'

'Never mind. Now, Mr Halliday, tell us about Mr Joe Patmore.'

'Joe worked here as a "brown coat", a kind of lab steward who'd unpack chemicals as they came in, look after the cleaning of the laboratory, that kind of thing. But he was caught stealing a quantity of hydrocyanic acid from this laboratory. Apparently he came back to the plant after we'd closed for the day. We don't have night shifts here. The security man saw him, with a mask over his face, decanting some of the acid into a bottle, which he then stoppered. Bill Simpson — that's the security man — let him leave the premises so that Patmore could be clearly seen as a thief, and followed him. He'd already alerted the local police on his phone.

'Before Patmore had gone a few yards the police arrived in a squad car, all guns blazing, but there was no sign of the loot on him. He must have passed it to an accomplice as soon as he left the factory. He denied it all, and said that Bill Simpson had misinterpreted what he'd seen, but no one who knows Bill would ever doubt his word. Mr Perry decided not to make a complaint, and the matter was dropped. But Joe Patmore got the sack.'

* * *

'Do you see the connection now?' asked Lance once they were settled back in the car.

'Why don't you just tell us?' asked Noel grumpily. 'You only ask us because you know we don't know. Stop gloating, will you, and *tell* us!'

'The clue is in the name Patmore,' said Lance. 'A Miss Patmore, who spent a pleasant week as a lodger in a B & B in West Deering, and went for a nice walk in the grounds of Holy Cross Abbey on the very day that the Reverend Julian Stringer was murdered. It was a kitchen knife for him, not poison, but I've no doubt that it was "Miss Patmore", i.e. Melanie Grint, who persuaded Joe Patmore to purloin that prussic acid. She may be a relative of his, or she may be more than that.'

'How are we going to find out?' asked Chloe.

'We'll ask him. I was almost a hundred per cent certain that the name Patmore would surface sooner or later, because I was convinced that the woman in the B & B was Melanie Grint, and that the assumed name of "Patmore" might be that of a friend or relative. I know where Joe Patmore is,' he concluded, 'so let's go and talk to him now.'

* * *

Joe Patmore lived in a house share in a small lane off Southwark Street. He was a pale-faced, stooping man with a white moustache forming a contrast to his still black hair. He received his visitors in his bedroom on the first floor, where he'd squeezed in a small sofa and a chair next to the bed. A judicious eye surveying his property and furnishings would soon conclude that Joe was only just keeping poverty at bay.

'Mel is a cousin of my father's sister's husband — at least, I think that's what she is. She's always been around, if you get my meaning. The Patmores always regarded her as one of them, but her name was actually Grint. She had a lot of mental trouble, and was locked up in a mental hospital for years before they let her out. She'd had a lot of tragedy in her life, I won't deny it, but she was a miserable sort of woman. Whenever she came into a room, the light seemed to fade. So what is it you want to know? If you want to know where she lives, well, I can't oblige you, because I don't know. She certainly doesn't live round here.'

'I want to know if you gave her a bottle of hydrocyanic acid, which you — er — obtained from your employer.'

'Yes, I did, and it cost me my job. It wasn't much, but it was a livelihood. Whenever Mel hovers in sight, misery follows in her wake.' In spite of himself, Joe Patmore laughed. 'She came to see me one day some months ago, and asked me whether I could get her a little bottle of HCL to get rid of a wasps' nest. I didn't think Mr Perry would mind all that much, but Bob the security man made a fuss, and the outcome was that I got the sack. Mel had come over from — from wherever she lives, and was waiting for me that night when I left the factory, and I gave her the bottle there and then. Good job, wasn't it? I wasn't found "in possession", as they say. So the police took no action.'

'Are you still out of work, Mr Patmore?' asked Lance Middleton.

'No, I'm working at Borough Market as a general dogsbody.' Again, that laugh. There seemed to be nothing self-pitying about this man.

'And you don't know where Melanie Grint can be found?'

'No, I don't. All I can tell you is, she doesn't live on this side of the river. She was a housekeeper to a vicar for years — the lady who got murdered with the very same stuff as I got for Melanie. But that was for wasps' nests. I can't see Mel murdering her employer. After all, when that vicar died, Mel was out of work. I think she must still be in London somewhere, but I can't say for certain. When she was in that lunatic asylum up north — Bury, or Bolton, somewhere like that — she chummed up with another patient there, a woman who'd had electric wires fastened into her brain, or something — anyway, they were both cured, and came back to London together. Maybe she's with *her*.'

Joe Patmore stopped speaking, and regarded Lance with a kind of gravely mocking air. Lance knew what this meant. He took out his wallet, and extracted a twenty-pound note, which he laid on the table.

'Now I come to think of it,' said Joe, 'her name was Susan Gledhill. Fancy my remembering that! All this was years ago. I don't know where you'll find Susan Gledhill, but she was a Londoner, and I'm sure she'll turn up somewhere, if you know where to look.'

As the three investigators made to leave, Lance, who was rearmost, turned back. 'Joe,' said Lance, 'can I have a private word with you?'

Noel and Chloe made their way to the car, and eventually Lance joined them.

'Susan Gledhill,' said Lance. 'I'm sure that Joe Patmore actually knows that those two women are holed up together somewhere, but he's not going to rat on them — not directly, at any rate. Just as he's not going to admit to himself that "Mel" murdered her employer. I think we're done here for the day.'

Chloe looked at her watch. 'I think most of the public records places will be closed by now, but I'll see if I can track down Susan Gledhill tomorrow — unless I can turn up something online tonight. Find Susan, and we'll find Melanie.'

'Lance,' said Noel Greenspan, 'what was that "private word" about? Or is it a deadly secret?'

'Oh, *that*. Well, Joe had a nice turn of phrase, and despite his misfortunes has retained his sense of humour. I've got a sort of network of informants and observers scattered all over London, and thought that Joe Patmore would be an interesting addition. He was quite taken with the idea of being a paid spy, and we shook hands on it.'

* * *

Late in the afternoon of the next day, Chloe returned from her research, and met Noel and Lance in Lance's chambers in Lincoln's Inn.

'Susan Gledhill is a woman of much the same age as Melanie,' said Chloe. 'I wasn't able to gain access to her medical records, of course, but I've turned up a few news items about her. Like Melanie, she was in service, a housekeeper to a retired stockbroker. Susan, like Melanie, was a good cook and gave every satisfaction to her employer. But after a while, she became convinced that the Devil was inhabiting the old man's body, and she could hear the voices of angels urging her to slay the Devil. So she purchased a meat cleaver, and chopped his head off.'

'Not very nice,' said Lance.

'No. She was unfit to plead, and I found that she was sent to the same mental hospital in Bolton where Melanie was confined. That's where she was subject to electro-convulsive therapy. It's quite unusual nowadays, but some hospitals do still use it for severe cases that haven't responded to other treatment.'

'All pals together,' said Noel. 'Two murderers, now living together somewhere in London, or maybe further afield—'

'No,' said Chloe, 'not all that far afield. I found a picture of her home in one of the newspaper articles, and located the exact address with the help of Google Maps. Susan Gledhill used to live in a place called Railway Lane, in Cricklewood. Number eighteen. I can't say for sure that she's still there, but it's worth a look.'

'Cricklewood,' said Lance. 'I know it quite well. It's a thriving London borough with a lot of Victorian terraces, and old villas standing in their own gardens. Quite a respectable place for a couple of killers to lie low in. It's time for us to pay Cricklewood a visit.'

12. OVERHEARD IN CRICKLEWOOD

Railway Lane, a quiet street of faded red-brick villas off Cricklewood Broadway, lay basking in the summer sun as Lance brought his car to a halt. Nobody was about.

Number eighteen looked innocuous enough, a solid two-storey villa with a plaque declaring '1861'. The front garden was overgrown, and the flowerbeds neglected. A battered Ford Escort stood on the drive.

'Now, Chloe,' said Lance Middleton, 'I want you to stay in the car while Noel and I beard these two murderous women in their den. I've not let Paul French know that we're here, because I'm not quite sure what we're going to say or do once we get inside that house. But I don't want you to be there, in case Susan tries a further attempt at decapitation, or Melanie offers us a nice cup of tea laced with cyanide. Noel and I are both, er, well-built fellows, who should be able to subdue a couple of lethal ladies if they turn nasty.'

Rather to Lance's surprise, Chloe raised no objection, and the two men walked up the path of number eighteen and rang the doorbell. Nobody answered. Lance tried the knocker, and after what seemed like a whole minute the door was cautiously opened. He saw a rather slatternly woman in her thirties, quite good-looking, but with a face lined with suffering. She had untidy blonde hair, and a hearing aid in her right ear.

'Yes?'

'Are you Susan Gledhill? I believe that Melanie Grint lives here with you? We'd like to have a word with her, if that's all right.'

Susan Gledhill didn't seem surprised. 'You'd better come in. Nobody calls here except for the milkman on Thursday. So I expect you're something to do with that poor vicar who was murdered.'

She stood aside to let the two men enter. They found themselves in a narrow hall, the floor covered with a worn strip of carpet. The house smelt stale. Everything was painted either cream or dull brown. A grandfather clock had stopped, and had never been rewound.

'Melanie, you've got visitors.'

She preceded them into a spacious sitting room at the back of the house, overlooking the rear garden. It was solidly furnished, but everything looked as though it dated back to the fifties of the last century.

So, thought Lance, *this is the Melanie that everybody talks about, but whom I've never seen. In contrast to her friend, she's dressed neatly, and evidently looks after herself well. But she seems very shy, and it's evidently a great effort for her to meet my gaze.*

'I'll make us some tea,' said Susan Gledhill, and Lance watched as she walked rather stiffly from the room. He wondered whether she had made tea for the old stockbroker before she decapitated him.

'Sit down, won't you, gentlemen,' said Melanie Grint. 'Nobody's bothered me since I left Rushbrooke Hill, after poor dear Stacey was murdered. But I suppose it was inevitable that all sorts of questions would be asked. I assume you *are* here about Stacey? How can I help you?'

A reasonable, measured tone of voice, thought Lance. So far, no signs of the fanatic about to break through her sober facade. He answered Melanie's question.

'Well, as I think you know, the killer of the Reverend Stacey Williams has still not been found, and we are trying to build up a picture of what she was like, what friends she may have had — anything that could give us a lead. The police investigations haven't been very successful, to say the least.'

'And who are you gentlemen?'

'My name is Lance Middleton, QC, and this is Noel Greenspan, who's a private detective. We've been hired by Colonel Calderdale to make private enquiries of our own.'

'Colonel Calderdale!' Melanie Grint spat the word out with what seemed like genuine vehemence. 'He persecuted Stacey from the moment she set foot in his parish, and when she was reduced to a tearful wreck — oh, yes, she put on a bold front for those people, but she knew that she could let herself go in front of me — with her confidence undermined, *he* came to the vicarage, thinking that they could kiss and make up! I wouldn't let him near her!'

Susan Gledhill came into the room carrying a tray holding four mugs of tea, a sugar bowl and a milk jug. Lance watched her as she put it down on a low table. She had strong, muscular arms, strong enough to hack a man's head off.

Noel was preoccupied with similar thoughts. Perhaps Melanie was going to orchestrate a double murder and a double suicide by means of doctored tea. But somehow, he doubted it. One thing he *did* know: he would have to keep a watch on Lance. He was a brilliant lawyer, but not a trained detective. Already he seemed to have succumbed to Melanie Grint's quiet, rather respectful, demeanour. But Melanie would have to get up early to put one over *him*.

The four of them sipped their tea in a rather embarrassed silence.

'Tell them about that mad clergyman, Mel,' said Susan, 'the one who put the pig's blood in the font to frighten her.'

'The Reverend Julian Stringer. He was a half-crazed lunatic with a bee in his bonnet about women not being able to be priests. He hung around the church, and he'd lurk in the vicarage grounds. Sometimes he'd follow *me* when I was out shopping in the village, muttering and murmuring, but he'd got the wrong one if he thought I was scared of him. I told him more than once to his face that I'd report him to the police for harassment.'

'Tell him about the blood, Mel. When you went to that farmer's place.'

'I used to go and buy bacon and black puddings from a local farmer,' said Melanie, 'and one day I saw that man Stringer lurking in the farm yard, near the shed where the farmer kept his store of pigs' blood. I saw him go into the shed, and come out almost straight away, holding something close to his chest under his coat. It was only when that terrible business happened with the font that I realised what he'd been doing.'

'He poured blood into the font to frighten Stacey,' said Susan Gledhill. 'He was a menace. And now we hear that he, too, was murdered in some kind of mental home for clergymen. One of the other residents did for him, I expect. When mentally disturbed people are all penned in together, terrible things can happen.'

Susan pushed the hair back from her forehead, and Lance saw the scarring produced by the electro-convulsive therapy that she had endured.

'Tell him about the keys,' said Susan.

'I had a duplicate key to the vestry,' said Melanie, 'which I hung on a hook in the vicarage kitchen. It was quite a big key, for a mortise lock. And then, one day, I left the usual key upstairs, so I took the duplicate and went across to the vestry door. But the key didn't fit. It was the *wrong* key. That showed how cunning Stringer was. He didn't just steal the key, he provided another one, knowing that I wouldn't notice for some time. I don't want to make wild accusations, and the man's dead, but I think that was how he got into the vestry some time on that Sunday morning, and poisoned that bottle of wine.'

Lance found himself all but mesmerised by Melanie's narrative. There was nothing hysterical or dramatic about her account of events. She seemed to speak with quiet authority. The whole case was being turned upon its head. Noel seemed to have gone into a kind of waking doze.

'He used to give them sweets,' said Melanie. 'The servers, I mean. And he gave Linda — that was one of the two girls — a lovely vanity case as a present. Both those girls liked him — Mary and Linda. They were too young to recognise evil, and thought he was just a funny old man. Stacey told them not to talk to him, ever, but young girls can be sly.'

Noel Greenspan was sitting in an armchair facing the back garden. He had been content to leave the questioning to Lance, the professional inquisitor, but his own interpretation of what the two women were saying was very different, he knew, to what Lance was thinking. Lance was falling under Melanie's quiet spell. Later, if they ever got out of the house alive, he'd cause the scales to fall from Lance's eyes.

Suddenly he saw something in the garden that set his heart pounding with fear. *Don't let the others see! Don't let Lance see! And please, God, don't let these two women turn round . . . Sip your tea, and calm down . . .*

'When it was all over,' Melanie continued, 'all I wanted to do was to get out of that place and come here to be with Susan. I'd always borne in mind that one day Stacey might not want my services any longer, and Susan was eager that I should come to live with her. We'd been through so much together, you see.'

'But you stayed on at the vicarage until Stacey's parents had visited,' said Lance.

'Yes, that was the least that I could do. I had been keeping house for Stacey for the last couple of years that she was at St John the Baptist, Paddington, so I knew Mr and Mrs Williams quite well. They were very devout in their own way, but quite a few people felt that they had not really wanted their daughter to enter the ministry. They were hoping that she would have trained as a lawyer. But there, Stacey knew her own mind, and went her own way. But there was a coolness between Stacey and her parents after that.'

'Did they ever visit her in any of her other parishes?' asked Lance.

'Oh, no. As I said, they'd never wanted her to enter the ministry at all. And when they came to see me at Rushbrooke Hill, they showed not the slightest interest in the church, or in the vicarage, for that matter. They rummaged through Stacey's things, and threw a lot of stuff out into the bins, and into some black bin bags. I hadn't the heart to open them and see what they'd thrown out.'

Lance wondered if their dislike of Stacey's vocation had made them throw away her Bible and prayer book.

Melanie's account of events had thrown a new and disturbing light upon the nature of the evidence in the case. It was time to go, and consider a reappraisal of the whole business.

'Well, thank you very much, Miss Grint,' he said, 'for talking to us today. I only wish you hadn't disappeared so quickly from Rushbrooke Hill before you could be questioned as to your view of events. It looks very much as though Julian Stringer plotted and carried out the murder of the woman he regarded as being possessed by a spirit. What you have told us today more or less confirms it.'

'It made it very difficult for me,' said Melanie, 'because if I had denounced him publicly, he could have then said that I was trying to cover up my own crime, because I had spent a long time in an asylum. You have no idea of the prejudice there is in society against people like Susan and me. So I judged it best to disappear from the scene, and leave the whole matter to the police.'

Susan Gledhill looked at her watch.

'You've got that dental appointment at twelve, Mel,' she said. 'It's a quarter past eleven.'

Lance got up from his chair, and Noel followed suit. Melanie stayed in the room, and Susan accompanied them to the front door.

'I hope that will be the end of this business,' she said. 'Melanie needs to be left in peace.'

* * *

As soon as they were back in the car Noel burst into speech.

'You let that woman mesmerise you, Lance! I was watching you! Her anti-Calderdale rant was to be expected, but everything else she said was a pack of carefully crafted lies. Why did she claim Stringer had given those two girls sweets and presents? Even a child of thirteen would refuse a costly vanity case from a frightening old man that she'd been warned about. The whole object of that lie was to suggest that Linda was open to bribery, just in case one of them had seen something they shouldn't.'

'Yes, I suppose you're right. But—'

'Let me finish, Lance. You notice how her pal Susan fed her the material? "Tell him about this, tell him about that." And so we come to her refinements on the wicked ways of Julian Stringer. First, she said that she'd seen him lurking around the sheds at Hinton's farm. I thought she did that very well, openly admitting that she bought produce from the farm, just in case anyone in the future remembered having seen her there on occasion. It was a lie. Poor Stringer was genuinely horrified about the profanation of the font.

'And then she told us the story of the missing duplicate key, making it possible to believe that Stringer had been able to gain access to the vestry in order to poison the wine. All accusations against a man who was safely dead. Then, to cap it all, Melanie suggested that Stringer had been murdered by a fellow inmate of Holy Cross Abbey.

'A splendid tissue of lies, and I watched you lapping it all up! Melanie is a clever, crafty woman, and a seamless liar, ably prompted by Susan. It was Melanie, calling herself Miss Patmore, who stayed at the B & B in West Deering and went out one fine morning to stab Julian Stringer in the back.'

'I stand corrected,' said Lance, glumly. 'I was preening myself on how clever I was when I took you to the plastics factory in Rotherhithe. Now I'm making amends here in Cricklewood. Why did she murder Stringer?'

'This is only a guess, but I think he might have seen her pouring the pigs' blood into the font. Maybe she thought he

143

might pop up one day to try a bit of blackmail. Well, dead men tell no tales. Underneath that mild exterior I sense that there's a very frightened, unbalanced personality lurking.'

'And all that talk about Stacey's parents—'

'All that talk, Lance, was a very effective demolition of the integrity of Stacey's parents by suggesting that they never really wanted her to be ordained. She tried to hint that it was the Williamses who threw their daughter's Bible and prayer book away. Can you for one lucid moment believe that? She was cunning enough not to make mention of that letter concerning Gregory Standish. Melanie wanted the contents of that letter to become known, as a means of blackening Stacey's name after her death. But it was a mistake. What parent, coming across such a letter about their dead daughter, would simply tear it across, and throw it away? They would have taken it with them, and destroyed it at home. So there you have it, Lance.

'But let's change the subject, so as to spare you further embarrassment. Have you noticed that Chloe's not here in the car?'

'Yes, I did notice. I expect she got tired of waiting and went for a walk,' said Lance, rather lamely.

'No, she didn't go for a walk. While you were listening to Melanie's lies,' said Noel, 'I saw to my horror that Chloe was creeping up to the house along a path bordering the back lawn. I might have known that she wouldn't just sit there meekly. She somehow got into the garden, and I've no doubt whatever that she's in the house at this very moment, listening to what the two ladies are talking about.'

'What should we do?'

'Drive the car further up the road, where they won't see it. I'll switch my phone on, and when Chloe's good and ready, she'll give us a call. Unless, of course, the two ladies have already murdered her, though I doubt that.'

Lance did as he was bid, and presently they saw the two women emerge from their house and get into their Ford Escort. In a moment they had reversed into the road, and driven off, presumably to Melanie's dentist.

Noel's phone rang. It was Chloe, asking whether the coast was clear. Soon after this she emerged from the front door of the house, and joined her two friends in the car.

* * *

'I had no intention of sitting there meekly in the car,' said Chloe, 'while my two heroes braved those homicidal harpies. No, I had a plan of my own.'

The three investigators had returned to Lance Middleton's chambers in Lincoln's Inn, where the two men gave Chloe a full account of what Susan and Melanie had told them.

'I think I must have been mesmerised by that woman,' Lance admitted ruefully. 'She was so calm, cool and collected. But Noel soon disabused me once we'd got safely out of the house.'

'I saw you creeping up that path at the side of the garden,' said Noel. 'Seeing you there scared me out of my wits.'

'There was a side passage two houses away to the left. It came out on to an allotment facing the back walls of the houses in Railway Lane. Most of the back gates had the house numbers written on them, including number eighteen. It was unlocked, and I slipped through into the back garden. I won't go into details about how I got into the house — Noel will know what I would have done, but you, Lance, would only be embarrassed. I could hear you all talking in that back room, so I looked around for a cupboard or cloakroom, found one, and hid in there. I heard you being shown the door by Susan, who hoped that people would leave poor Melanie alone in future.'

'I was terrified that they'd hear you, or just sense that there was somebody there,' said Noel.

'Well, they didn't, and I crept out of the cupboard and stood outside the door of that back room, which was partly ajar. And I heard everything that they said. They spent a few moments cackling like a couple of hens, and then one of them said, "I could have told that fat freak anything and he would have believed it. The other one, the so-called detective, just sat there and dozed off."

'"You did very well," said Susan, "especially when you laid all the blame on that pathetic clergyman. I think that just about wraps the whole business up. But you did for him, didn't you, just like you did for the vicar."'

'She confessed to both murders?' cried Noel. 'Why, then, we've got her!'

'Don't be too sure about that, Noel,' said Lance. 'An able defence counsel could make mincemeat of all this in court. You heard Susan say that Melanie had murdered the vicar, but you didn't hear Melanie herself make such a confession. And that's setting aside the issue of unlawful entry. But go on, Chloe, what else did they say?'

'"Why did you murder him, Melanie?" said Susan.

'"I got rid of him because I'm convinced that he saw me pouring that blood into the font. He was always sneaking around that church. He was a danger, you see, and I couldn't rest until I'd got rid of him. It was quite easy. I went and stayed in a bed and breakfast near to that so-called abbey until the time was ripe for me to find him taking a walk in the garden. It was a gamble, I suppose, but the landlady had told me that the patients nearly always took a walk in the garden every day. He heard me approaching, and turned round. 'What do you want?' he cried. 'Away with you, energumen!' He turned to run back to the house, and I stabbed him in the back with a steak knife."

'"Energumen? What does that mean?" Susan asked.

'"It's what that old fool used to call Stacey. It means a woman possessed by a demon. Maybe he was right. I think he *was* right about Stacey. If ever a woman was possessed by the Devil, *she* was! Anyway, we're rid of him now, and in a couple of weeks' time we'll be rid of the lot of them."'

'Did she give any details about Stacey?' asked Lance.

'No, she didn't mention her again. But she went on to say something that made my blood run cold. "There's one more mouth to stop," she said, "somebody down in the Borough. You know who I mean. With him gone, you and I can start afresh." I heard them get up from their chairs, then, and beat a hasty but careful retreat to the cupboard. When I was sure that they'd gone, I phoned you. And there it is.'

'I think that was a very brave thing to do, Chloe,' said Lance. 'And it leaves us in no doubt that Melanie Grint is a deranged killer who is still on the loose. And she called me a fat freak?'

'She did, but I'm sure you'll agree that her description was both inaccurate and excessive.'

'Yes, yes indeed. It's time for us to let DI French and DS Edwards know all this, and for the police, or better still, us three, to keep a constant watch over Melanie Grint and Susan Gledhill. They plan to make a move — possibly abroad, but first, Melanie has business to do in the Borough. You know what that means, don't you?'

'Well, er—'

'It means, Noel, that she's after poor Joe Patmore, the man who furnished her with the hydrocyanic acid which she used to murder Stacey Williams. Joe works in Borough Market, as he told us when we visited him. And Joe is now one of my little coterie of observers. I think, if we are very careful, that we can arrange for our Melanie to walk into a nicely contrived trap.'

13. MELANIE'S VISIT

A muggy wet day. Melanie Grint turned out of Southwark Street into the lane where Joe Patmore lived in his shared house. Joe liked lager, and she had brought a couple of bottles of Budweiser in a plastic shopping bag to share with him. He wouldn't say no to a nice refreshing drink mid-morning. Poor Joe! He'd never had much, and no one would really miss him.

She knocked on the door, which was opened by a middle-aged woman in faded jeans and a top adorned with a picture of Elvis.

'Is Joe about?'

'You'd better come in. You're lucky finding Joe in today. The others are all out. There's only him and me here.'

The woman led Melanie up the narrow, dark staircase to the first floor. It was a gloomy place, she thought, and could do with a good cleaning by the look of things. The landing was lit by a single forty-watt lamp bulb.

'Joe?' said the woman, knocking on a door to the right of the stairs, 'you've got a visitor.' She pushed open the door, and Melanie came face-to-face with what she hoped would be her final victim. He was sitting in a chair beside the empty fireplace, reading the *Daily Mirror*.

'Come in, Melanie,' said Joe Patmore. 'I got your note. We don't often see you in this part of the world. Sit down. What have you got there, in the Tesco bag?'

'A couple of Buds, Joe. I thought we'd have a nice drink and a chat. I want to tell you what Susan and I have decided to do.'

Joe got up and opened a cupboard. He returned with two beer glasses. She put the two bottles on the table, together with a bottle opener. *Remember: His is the one with the little pencilled cross on the label.*

'So what are you two going to do, then, Mel?'

'We're going to leave London, and go to Scotland, where nobody's ever heard of us. Susan's selling that house, and we've both got quite a bit put by. We—'

The door suddenly opened, and the woman with the Elvis top said, 'I'm just going down the off-licence, Joe. Look after the house while I'm out!'

'Doesn't that woman ever knock?' said Melanie angrily.

'Never mind her, she's harmless. So you're going up to Scotland? Well, that's very interesting. If I were you, I'd go there as soon as possible. I've had some people round here, asking questions. They'd found out that I was the one who got you the prussic acid to — to kill those wasps with.'

Joe suddenly began to laugh. 'Wasps?' he cried. 'Wasps, my eye!'

'Hush, you silly fool! Walls have ears. They'll hear you next door through the wall, so keep your voice down. Let's have a beer, and then I'll tell you all about Scotland.' She held a handkerchief to her mouth and nose while she opened the two bottles of Budweiser and poured them into the glasses. *Best get rid of him now, while the house is empty.*

'Got a cold, have you? Or is it hay fever?' Joe began to laugh again. He seemed disinclined to drink his beer. Melanie suddenly felt threatened; but what could this broken-down casual labourer do to her? Why should he do anything at all?

'Is my beer full of cyanide, like the bottle of wine that you used to poison Stacey Williams? Or have you brought a steak knife to kill me with, like you used on that mad clergyman?'

'How did you—? You know too much for your own good, Joe. Be careful.'

Joe Patmore's mocking tones were suddenly replaced by something more harsh and intimidating.

'So, you two are off to Scotland, are you? Well, Susan will get a good price for that house of hers, and I want my share of it as the price for keeping silent. You hunted that vicar down, didn't you, because of all the rotten things she'd done to Margaret your sister, and to poor Jim, and refusing to christen little Ellie? You must have been off your rocker! But your secret's safe with me, as long as I get my cut of whatever's going.'

There it was again, the cold hatred that had sustained her in her pursuit of Stacey was welling up again, this time against this sneering, pathetic little man who thought she would buy his silence. She had come to get rid of him, and as the cyanide trick had not worked, she would find some other means of killing him. Her eyes darted round the room to look for suitable items that she could use as a weapon. Could she launch a sudden attack, now he was on to her? Joe was all bluster. She was an adept at removing people who threatened her security. And yes, if there was nothing suitable in the room, there was a steak knife at the bottom of the Tesco bag.

'There's nothing but beer in that bottle,' she said.

'Oh, yes, I don't think! You're mad. You were always mad. You had no cause to murder that woman, or the clergyman. You ought to be locked up. That gentleman, that Mr Middleton, QC, knows more about you than you can imagine.'

'Does he?' Melanie cried in a sudden passion. 'And what does *he* know about life? People like that know nothing about the burdens that working-class people have to bear. Tragedies that couldn't be prevented, just for the lack of a couple of hundred pounds. Debts mounting up, bailiffs at the door . . . This country's awash with money, but only a fraction of it seeps down to working people.'

'People like them?' said Joe. 'What do you mean by that?'

'I mean people like that fat detective, making a cushy living by snooping into people's private lives in return for cash. People like his friend the well-padded QC, making a fortune in the law courts, feeding off the greed of people trying to overturn wills, and grab what they can of dead people's goods. There are thousands of them, well-dressed and well-fed, dining at The Ritz while other people are queuing up outside food banks . . .'

Melanie suddenly stopped, and seemed to recollect herself. When she spoke next, it was with a confiding tone, as if she was telling of her innermost secrets to a close friend; but she had no friend in that room, or in that house.

'But there are worse sinners than that lot, Joe Patmore — far worse, and Stacey Williams was one of them. Yes, I killed her, and I'm not sorry for it. She was an affront to humanity. You seem to have forgotten it all, if indeed you ever knew half the truth of it. So you sit there, Joe, and listen while I remind you what this was all about.

'I'm going to take you back in time to 2010, when that woman was vicar of St John the Baptist, Paddington. There were a lot of poor, struggling people there, people who tried their best to help each other with what little they had.

'I wasn't there at that time, I was still locked up in that place in Bolton, way up north, as I expect you know. But my sister, Margaret Dwyer, came to visit me as often as she could. Her husband, Jim, was a roofer, but he suffered from chronic bronchitis, and was out of work more often than not, living on benefits. He was a decent, quiet man, and he and Margaret got on well together.'

Melanie Grint had forgotten that she was confessing to Joe. She was reliving the past as though it was vividly present.

'They only had that one child, Ellie, who was the light of Jim's life. I never saw her in the flesh, on account of being confined to the hospital, but Margaret would bring me photographs to see. A lovely little girl she was, a toddler, with blonde curls. The Dwyers weren't regular churchgoers, but they'd turn up at Easter and Christmas, and at the summer garden fête. People told me all this later. What's that noise? Is there somebody else in this house?'

Melanie flung open the door and looked out on to the landing.

'There's nobody there,' said Joe. 'Tell me more about Jim Dwyer.'

'Jim had a friend, another roofer, who attended another church in the neighbourhood, Sion Chapel, it was called, and this friend asked Jim whether Ellie had been baptised. When he said no, this friend told him that if Ellie died unbaptised, she'd go to hell, and that he'd better get the vicar to baptise her as soon as possible.

'Margaret told me what happened after the tragedy. She and Jim went to see the local vicar, who was Stacey Williams, and asked her to baptise little Ellie. She agreed, of course, but she turned what should have been a straightforward half-hour's work into an obstacle race. She said that they'd have to come to church every Sunday for the next three weeks, and find a couple of godparents. They'd have to attend a couple of evening talks about the meaning of baptism, and so on and so forth. A lot of it went over their heads, I expect, but kowtowing to people in authority — people like the *vicar* — was second nature to both of them. So they did everything that Little Miss Bossy Boots told them.

'And then, one night, Ellie fell into convulsions and died. It was bad enough for Margaret, but Jim was frantic with grief.'

'I know all this,' said Joe. 'Or most of it, at any rate.'

'No, you don't!' cried Melanie, half rising from her chair. 'You know nothing! You know nothing about the pain, the almost physical agony that those two endured. And it got worse. Jim became convinced that Ellie had gone to hell. And as a result of that conviction he hanged himself. Margaret sold up, then, and came to live near me, in Bolton. She looked as though she'd aged ten years. She was ill, shattered. And then she told me what Stacey had done, something that made me determined to seek revenge on her for the deaths of Ellie and Jim, and the suffering endured by my sister, who died of cancer the next year.

'That woman was evil! If ever anyone was possessed by a demon, it was Stacey Williams, and the more I got to know her, the more convinced I became that she was a limb of Satan. Julian Stringer sensed that, too, and made no bones about telling anyone who cared to listen. But nobody did. She rode roughshod over everyone she came across. Everybody said how wonderful she was, but all the changes she made were for her own satisfaction, and if anyone got in the way she would get rid of them.

'And then a few days after she'd settled in Bolton, Margaret came to see me in the hospital, and told me what Stacey had done with the bodies of Jim and Ellie. He was to be buried in the "suicide's plot", as she called the north side of the church. And she refused to bury Ellie at all. Well, the archdeacon and the Bishop of London heard about that, and made her take a holiday while a decent young curate came and buried Jim and Ellie in the one grave. That's how hard and inhuman that woman was. She lived by rigid rule books about church doctrine and practice, and woe betide anyone who broke the rules! And yet, all through her life, she'd left a trail of death and ruin behind her.'

'It was terrible, I know that, Mel. She shouldn't have done any of that.'

'I'm glad to hear you say so. So I managed to get the job as her housekeeper in the last couple of years that she was at Paddington. I looked after her well, and she began to confide in me. It was all about *me*, *me*, she never thought for one moment that other people could have been hurt by her actions. To the outside world I seemed fiercely devoted to her, but I had, in fact, got her completely in my power, and I was waiting for the right time to get revenge for what she had done to my family.

'I hated her,' Melanie continued, 'but I clung to her like a limpet. She moved from Paddington to a very nice living in the country, and I went with her, and from there she went to Rushbrooke Hill. She took it for granted that I would go there, too. She never thought to ask me, and I intended to go with her anyway. She'd reached the stage where she couldn't do without me, you see. And it was there that I judged the time was right to send her packing to the Devil, who she'd served so very well.'

She stopped talking when they both heard the urgent siren of an ambulance, or perhaps a police car, drawing up in a nearby street.

'I don't understand how a clergywoman could be an agent of the Devil,' Joe said. 'You'll be saying next that she performed a Black Mass, like in those horror films.'

He stretched out his hand to the glass of beer, and Melanie held her breath for a second. But no. He'd thought better of it and sat back in his chair, shaking his head, and grinning at her as though she was a fool.

'Listen,' she said, 'that woman worshipped herself. "Our Stacey, which art on earth." She was a walking blasphemy, if you're not too thick to understand what I mean by that. She made a mockery of everything that the Bible teaches. So maybe I was sent to punish her, and to exorcise her.

'When I was in the psychiatric hospital in Bolton, the local Anglican vicar used to visit me once a week, and listening to him, I realised that the Church of England had a lot of good, faithful ministers in it. He was one of them. He was very High Church, just like Stacey, and he told me a lot of things, in a quiet, confiding way, that I'd never known before. He told me that there were two sacraments, baptism and Holy Communion, both very sacred, because they were instituted by Christ Himself.'

'I've never heard you talk like this before, Mel,' said Joe. 'You seem to have developed the gift of the gab. You certainly know how to tell a story.'

'That's because I received a good education,' said Mel. 'Did you know that I went to the local grammar school? I left at sixteen with five GCSEs, three of them grade A. They wanted me to stay on to do A levels, but you know how poor we all were. In those days you left school and found a job to help out. There *is* someone out there!'

Melanie flung open the door, and went out on to the landing, flinging open the doors of the other bedrooms and going halfway down the stairs to peer down at the hallway. Nobody was about. She was soon back with Joe in his room.

'No, there's no one there. This empty house is giving me the jitters. What was I telling you? Oh, yes, getting a job to help out.

'I began to fancy that a woman who worked with me in a works canteen was casting spells on me to make me sick and miss my shifts. One day, I attacked her, and beat her up so badly that she had to go to hospital. That's when I was diagnosed with persecution mania, and was sent to Bolton.

'Anyway, that vicar told me all about baptism and Holy Communion, and it opened my eyes to how wicked Stacey Williams had been. By refusing to baptise little Ellie, she had profaned the sacrament of baptism, which she's no right to withhold from anyone, and that's why, when I came with her to Rushbrooke Hill, I put that pigs' blood in the font. "Flesh with the life thereof, which is the blood thereof, shall ye not eat." Genesis chapter nine, verse four. It was a way of getting my own back for what she did to Ellie. By not baptising her, she had profaned the font. I just paid her back in kind.'

Joe Patmore stirred restlessly. 'You could have made away with her in the vicarage,' he said. 'Why did you arrange to kill her at the altar? That was horrible. Everybody thought so, Mel, even non-religious people.'

'Don't you get it? For years and years she'd profaned the sacrament of Holy Communion, too. So I decided to cut her off in her sins at the altar itself. Every Mass she celebrated was a blasphemy, so I made her become her own executioner. And when she'd gone, I chucked her Bible and prayer book into the rubbish. No other unsuspecting minister was going to soil his hands on them if I could help it.'

Melanie laughed, and Joe felt his blood run cold.

'And then someone in the village chucked a brick through the window when she decided to rip all the old pews out of the church. That's when I wrote those poison pen letters, and just left them on the hall floor, where Stacey would find them. Julian Stringer was a godsend. I could blame everything on *him*, and he was vain enough or mad enough to believe at times that he'd done things that I'd done myself. But he saw me put the blood in the font. He wasn't a very nice man, anyway — nobody misses him. I went to stay in the village where he was hiding out, calling myself "Miss Patmore". No offence to you, Joe, but after all it's one of our family names.'

Joe got up from his chair, and the *Daily Mirror* slipped off his knees and on to the floor. 'You murdered the two of them! All this story about Ellie and the others is just a cover-up. You're mad, Melanie. You've always been mad.'

'Yes, I murdered the two of them!' Melanie cried. 'And now it's going to be your turn, Joe. You know too much, you've guessed too much, and you've heard too much.'

Without taking her eyes off Joe, Melanie Grint reached into her bag.

14. A STORMY NIGHT IN SUMMER

Melanie Grint sprang from her chair, and at the same time the door burst open and two uniformed police officers rushed into the room.

Melanie began to scream, and struggled to free herself from the vice-like grip of one of the police officers, who continued to caution her. Joe put his hands to his ears. If all this bedlam carried on much longer, he'd end up as mad as Melanie . . .

The screaming suddenly stopped, and Melanie became unnaturally calm. Her eyes seemed to glaze over. She didn't resist as she was led from the room.

'How are you, Joe? Are you all right?'

Joe sighed with relief as Lance Middleton came into the room.

'Yes, I'm all right. But I thought I'd had it for a moment when Mel went for that plastic bag. I was scared stiff. Mel seems to have been a dab hand with the steak knife.'

'Well, Joe, what you need is something nourishing to eat. Is there anywhere round here that does food?'

'There's the Duke of Wellington, a stone's throw from here. It's not the Ritz, but—'

'It'll do for us. Come on, Joe, let's get out of here.'

* * *

'The police and I heard everything, Joe,' said Lance. 'I must say, you have a flair for keeping a witness talking.'

'I just felt that I had to,' said Joe, 'but at the same time I was sorry for her. She's had an awful life, all things considered, and now it's come to this.'

Lance Middleton and Joe Patmore were enjoying gammon and chips in the Duke of Wellington pub. Although a renowned gourmet, Lance had eclectic tastes in food. All he asked was that everything was properly cooked. The gammon was excellent, and so were the chips.

'Your glass of beer will be found to contain a lethal dose of cyanide, but you'd guessed that already. You might say it was the case of the biter bit. After all, you supplied the prussic acid, so Melanie had saved a few drops of it for *you*.'

'She was going to murder me,' said Joe, 'just as she'd murdered Stacey, and that poor clergyman. And yet I still feel sorry for her!'

'She came to her senses as they were getting her into the ambulance,' said Lance. 'And the first thing she said was, "See that poor Susan's all right. She had nothing to do with any of this." My colleagues and I had already met Susan, and have been in contact with social services. They're going to send some people out there to see what they can do for her.'

'Didn't she cut somebody's head off?'

'She did. I've made some enquiries about Susan Gledhill. She was found guilty but insane, and was sent to live in a special unit up in Bolton. Well, after she underwent electro-convulsive surgery, the memory of that whole episode was burnt out of her brain. Quite literally, you know. She remembers nothing of the whole business.'

'What'll happen to Melanie?'

'We'll have to see. She'll be charged with murder, of course, initially the murder of Stacey Williams. And she'll have to appear before a judge and specialist counsel to determine whether she's fit to plead or not. That decision lies with the Crown Prosecution Service. So we'll have to see what the police are going to do. But one thing's certain, Joe. Hospital or prison, Melanie Grint will never be at liberty again.'

* * *

When Lance Middleton visited the house in Maida Vale where Stacey Williams's parents lived, he found it still attractive, and the gardens well-tended. But he thought that Elizabeth Williams had aged perceptibly since they had last met, and Stanley Williams looked as though he had been ill. Fresh flowers stood on the grand piano near to the framed photographs of Stacey.

'It's only now sinking in, Mr Middleton, that Stacey's gone,' said her father. 'We know she's in heaven and all that, but we so much wish that she was here with us. When she was very young, she was thinking about doing a degree in law, and going on to become a barrister. One of the other girls in her form at school did that. But . . .'

'Oh, if only she had!' cried Stacey's mother. 'She would have been so fitted to that — she would have made an excellent lawyer. If she'd done that, she'd still be with us, now!'

'And that woman, I hope she rots in prison,' said Stanley Williams. 'Mad be damned! She was pure evil.'

'We have a villa in Spain,' said Elizabeth Williams. 'We're thinking of selling up here, and retiring there. There are too many sad memories here, now. And it would be good for Stanley's health. He's — he's not as well as he should be.'

Lance Middleton had brought a briefcase with him, which he now opened.

'I have here Stacey's Bible, which you presented to her,' he said. He recalled the inscription on the fly-page: *For Stacey, from Mummy and Daddy*. 'And here's the prayer book that was given to her by the Bishop of London when she was ordained priest. The police found them somewhere in the empty vicarage.'

'Oh, I'm so glad!' cried Elizabeth, stretching out her hands to receive the books. 'We looked for them everywhere, didn't we, Stanley? Thank you so much for bringing them!'

Lance had not the heart to tell them that Stacey's books had been thrown out into the rubbish as a last vindictive act against her by Melanie Grint. Some things were best forgotten. When he left them, they came as far as the gate, waving as he drove away.

* * *

A week after Melanie Grint's arrest, DI Paul French received a letter from his friend Dr John Miller.

> *I thought you'd like to know that next Monday we're meeting to choose a new vicar for Holy Trinity, Rushbrooke Hill. Let's hope that Nigel Calderdale doesn't have a relapse! But that was an unkind thing to write. Nigel has assured me that he'll accept our choice without any fuss and bother, and I believe him. I find that he had hired those private eyes to assist in the investigation — you will have known that, of course. Well, they turned up trumps.*
>
> *We've narrowed down the shortlist to four, two men and two women, all highly qualified and experienced, and I was surprised that so many clergy applied for the post, considering what happened in the parish during the incumbency of the late Reverend Stacey Williams. The applications arrived on Alan Shirtcliffe's mat within days of Melanie Grint's arrest.*
>
> *Anyway, Nigel's got other things to occupy his mind at the moment, including his forthcoming marriage to Rose Talmadge, who has shown her own pleasure at the prospect of becoming mistress of Rushbrooke House by attacking Nigel's rather gloomy gardens with gusto. It's quite romantic in an old-fashioned way, and will expand Nigel's mind a lot, showing him that there's much more to life than Church politics and obscure theology.*
>
> *At Evensong last week we had psalm 91, the one that talks about 'the pestilence that walketh in darkness', and I recalled that occasion when Stacey had quoted it to me, giving*

me not only the English words but the Latin: negotium per-
ambulans in tenebris. Little did she realise that it was not
so much the Devil, though he was lurking around, but her
trusted housekeeper and confidante who was the pestilence. I
wonder whether Melanie Grint will be found insane? I'm no
expert in the field of insanity, but I can certainly say that
she was not normal.

Paul French picked up the telephone and got through
to John Miller.

'Is that you, John? I've just read your letter. You're not
the only one hinting at a plea of insanity, but it's not going
to happen. I've already spoken to various people. Although
it's not public knowledge yet, she's been judged fit to plead.
Moira's pleased no end.'

'Who were the "various people" you talked to?'

'Never you mind. No names, no pack drill. The lawyer
assigned to her case tried to introduce a plea of insanity, but
two independent psychiatrists said that while she had psy-
chological problems, she was clinically sane. That's what I'm
ringing you about. She's *sane*, John, and just plain wicked.
And she'll go to prison for the rest of her life.'

'There was some talk of a friend helping her do it — is
that right?'

'A distant relative got her the cyanide, but he thought
it was just for wasps. He helped the police catch her, and
he's got a very good lawyer, so it sounds as if he'll avoid
charges.'

'I was thinking of a woman.'

'Susan Gledhill? Just a housemate, as far as we can prove,
though the private investigators tell me she knew more about
Melanie's crimes than that suggests. But she can't be charged
with anything. She's still under the aftercare of the NHS, so
they'll be stepping up to make sure she's coping with the loss
of her friend.'

* * *

Dr John Miller put the phone down. So, he thought, that's the end of the affair. Nobody would clap eyes on Melanie again, and good riddance.

Paul French's implied strictures on his own views were justified. By mentioning the possibility of an insanity plea, he had been subconsciously looking for a way out for that woman. Well, Paul was right. Compassion should never be carried to excess. Melanie Grint cold-bloodedly murdered Julian Stringer on the suspicion that he had seen her pouring blood into the font. And her murder of Stacey Williams was positively diabolical.

A new vicar would arrive soon, and life would continue, he well knew: baptisms, holy days and festivals would unfold as they always had. People were starting to behave as though nothing had happened at all. But, deep down, no one in Rushbrooke Hill would ever forget what had happened to their vicar.

* * *

DI Paul French invited Chloe McArthur and Noel Greenspan to call upon him at Jubilee House. These two, he thought, were becoming an essential part of the law enforcement system in Oldminster. They had played a crucial role in the last four major investigations, and here they were again, fresh from their part in bringing Melanie Grint to justice.

'I've asked you here today,' said Paul French, 'to tell you about a police raid we carried out last week. This will be of particular interest to you, Chloe. For some years now we've had our eye on the Fellowship of Capricorn. I believe you had an interview with the Master of the Goat Herd?'

'I did. And I have to admit that he frightened the life out of me. He was decidedly a larger-than-life character. He said that he'd welcome me into his flock. He was after my money, or rather he was after the fictional money that I told him I had, but I hadn't, if you see what I mean.'

'He's a man who has thrived on his mesmerising personality,' said French, 'and his skill at using all kinds of fakery to deceive gullible people into parting with their cash. The Master of the Goat Herd is a man called Cyril Gage, a confidence trickster who has a record for obtaining money by false pretences, usually from elderly women with more money than sense, and young men who have lived dissolute lives, and want somewhere to lie low. They found that sanctuary at the old Tudor mansion in Mosspit Lane.'

'And you raided him?'

'Yes, we did, Chloe, and we found all the usual paraphernalia of fake mediums and the like. But we uncovered much more than that. Gage's main line of business was forging bank notes, and our raid discovered a first-class printing press in the cellar. The whole lot of them were taken into custody, and some of the weaker brethren have thrown Cyril Gage to the wolves. His trial for fraud and forgery is set for this coming September.'

'Adele Starkadder will be pleased,' said Chloe. 'It must have been very vexing for her to be living near to a fraudulent psychic, considering that she's a real one.'

'Is there such a thing?' asked Paul French, smiling.

'I used to doubt it,' said Chloe, 'but having met Adele Starkadder, I've changed my views.'

'Incidentally,' said DI French,' I've heard from my friend Dr John Miller that they've finally chosen a new vicar for Rushbrooke Hill. They—'

At that moment the phone rang.

'Yes, sir. At once, sir. I'll do that straight away.'

He put the phone down again, and stood up.

'That was the superintendent. I'll have to go now. Congratulations to both of you once again for helping to bring Melanie Grint to justice. And by the way,' he said, as he went into the corridor, 'the new vicar is someone called . . .' His voice was drowned out by a sudden blare of sirens as a couple of police cars drew to a halt in front of Jubilee House.

* * *

One stormy night in late summer, Lance Middleton, QC sat in his cosy chambers in Lincoln's Inn, listening to the rain beating against the windows, and congratulating himself on not being out. It had turned chilly, and a small fire burnt in the grate. He was reading a law report and sipping a glass of one of his choice brandies.

There came a knock on his door, and when he opened it he was surprised to see the rain-sodden figure of Noel Greenspan standing in the passage. He ushered him in, relieved him of his wet coat, and sat him down near the fire.

'Have a glass of brandy, Noel,' he said. 'And then tell me what brings you out on such a night as this. Didn't Shakespeare say something like that?'

'He did,' said Noel. 'In *The Merchant of Venice*. But I'm not here to bandy quotations, Lance. I was summoned up to London this morning by some people I know in Scotland Yard, who took me out to Belwood Women's Prison, where Melanie Grint is serving her sentence. They were very non-committal on the long drive out to Belwood, but once we got there, the warden met us at the gate, and it was from her that I learnt that Melanie Grint was dead.'

The two men sat in silence, listening to the growing storm raging outside in Lincoln's Inn Fields.

'I wondered, you know,' said Lance. 'I wondered whether she'd just sit there passively for the rest of her life. I assume that some visitor or other brought her the poison — for poison it must have been. Unless, of course, some other prisoner had a grudge against her, and murdered her in turn.'

'You're running ahead of yourself, Lance,' said Noel. 'When she was found dead in prison at six thirty this morning, the warden and her cohorts sprang into action. They thought as you did, you see: either suicide or murder. In either case there would be a rigorous enquiry. No, three doctors descended upon Belwood, carried Melanie Grint's body off to the police mortuary, and did an immediate autopsy. Melanie Grint died from a ruptured cerebral aneurism.'

Noel sipped his brandy. So she died alone in her cell, and from natural causes. In past times, they would have said that she'd cheated the gallows, but there were no gallows to cheat these days. Had she seen the ghosts of Stacey Williams and Julian Stringer, waiting to give their evidence before the heavenly tribunal? Probably not.

Don't speculate on these matters while Lance is around, Noel told himself. *He'll think you've gone mad.*

Sheets of vivid lightning were followed by crashing thunder.

'You'd better stay the night here, Noel,' said Lance. 'There's a snug guest room behind that door over there.'

He saw Noel Greenspan visibly relax, and joined him at the fireside.

'I was thinking about the big cases we've both been involved with over the last few years,' said Lance. 'The business of Sir Frank Renfield, the murder of Sir Frank Taylor, the decidedly creepy case of Bridget Messiter, and the Rembrandt Gallery affair. There was a lot of danger, and quite a bit of heartbreak, but those investigations were exciting and stimulating. Do you think there might be more to come?'

'I'm sure there will be,' said Noel. 'We'll lure you down to Oldminster again in the future, to partake of Chloe's cordon bleu delights. Oldminster's getting to be a hotbed of crime and villainy.'

It was just striking twelve when the friends decided to call it a day, and retired to their rooms. The storm continued to rage outside, but they both slept well, dreaming of investigations to come.

THE END

THE JOFFE BOOKS STORY

We began in 2014 when Jasper agreed to publish his mum's much-rejected romance novel and it became a bestseller.

Since then we've grown into the largest independent publisher in the UK. We're extremely proud to publish some of the very best writers in the world, including Joy Ellis, Faith Martin, Caro Ramsay, Helen Forrester, Simon Brett and Robert Goddard. Everyone at Joffe Books loves reading and we never forget that it all begins with the magic of an author telling a story.

We are proud to publish talented first-time authors, as well as established writers whose books we love introducing to a new generation of readers.

We have been shortlisted for Independent Publisher of the Year at the British Book Awards three times, in 2020, 2021 and 2022, and for the Diversity and Inclusivity Award at the Independent Publishing Awards in 2022.

We built this company with your help, and we love to hear from you, so please email us about absolutely anything bookish at feedback@joffebooks.com

If you want to receive free books every Friday and hear about all our new releases, join our mailing list: www.joffebooks.com/contact

And when you tell your friends about us, just remember: it's pronounced Joffe as in coffee or toffee!

ALSO BY NORMAN RUSSELL

THE OLDMINSTER MYSTERIES